A Picture Perfect Childhood

Enhancing Your Child's Imagination and Education in 15 Minutes a Day

Cay Gibson

ISBN:
978-0-6151-7981-0

Cover design by Clare Mulderink

Published through:

Literature Alive!
Sulphur, LA 70663

Lulu ID# 1407482

This book is dedicated to the talented authors and illustrators who sow the seeds to our imagination and to all the children who reap the harvest.

The Children's Hour
by Henry Wadsworth Longfellow

Between the dark and the daylight,
When the night is beginning to lower,
Comes a pause in the day's occupations,
That is known as the Children's Hour.

My heartfelt "Thank you" to:
- Kathryn Mulderink, Karen Edmisten, Mary Machado, Angie McIntyre and her daughter Devin for editing, proofing, and giving suggestions on drafts of *A Picture Perfect Childhood.*
- Kathryn Mulderink and Kimberly Kane (especially that early morning phone call) for guiding me through the lay-out and publication process and never failing to give advice and support.
- Clare Mulderink for doing such beautiful work creating the book's cover.
- Shalome Westberg for helping extensively with the "Cooking with Literature" booklist.
- All readers who suggested book titles found in the various booklists.

Clipart, used in this book to give it a picture-perfect touch, was supplied as follows:
- WP Clipart: www.wpclipart.com
- Dover Publications: http://store.doverpublications.com/
- Permission granted by Florida Center for Instructional Technology: http://etc.usf.edu/clipart/sitemap/sitemap.htm
- Artwork on pages 8, 9, 11, 12 created by the talented Theodore Schluenderfritz.

TABLE OF CONTENTS

A Book
by Edgar Guest

"Now" - said a good book unto me -
"Open my pages and you shall see
Jewels of wisdom and treasures fine,
Gold and silver in every line,
And you may claim them if you but will
Open my pages and take your fill.

"Open my pages and run them o'er,
Take what you choose of my golden store.
Be you greedy, I shall not care -
All that you seize I shall gladly spare;
There is never a lock on my treasure doors,
Come - here are my jewels, make them yours!

"I am just a book on your mantel shelf,
But I can be part of your living self;
If only you'll travel my pages through,
Then I will travel the world with you.
As two wines blended make better wine,
Blend your mind with these truths of mine.

"I'll make you fitter to talk with men,
I'll touch with silver the lines you pen,
I'll lead you nearer the truth you seek,
I'll strengthen you when your faith grows weak -
This place on your shelf is a prison cell,
Let me come into your mind to dwell!"

My Mama Read to Me

At night my mama read to me—tales of princesses in beautiful dresses with flowing yellow hair.

In the daytime, my cotton sack dress became a beautiful gown. My short brown hair became a waterfall of liquid gold.

At night, my mama read to me---stories of fairy rings hidden in purple violets and ivy green.

In the daytime, I danced in the swamp grass. I fancied it was a flower-filled fairy ring.

At night my mama read to me---stories of knights strong and castles foreboding.

In the daytime, a knight saved me from the dark, dank, dirty walls of the enemy's rat-infested lair.

I asked my mama where all the stories came from. She said, "From the book lady."

I imagined the book lady to be a fairy tale princess. She was dressed in pink and bestowed richly crafted treasures to all her subjects.

I was away at Granny's house when the book lady brought more stories.

That night my mama read to me---stories of dungeons and dragons, three bears and a little Cajun girl called *Jolie Blonde.**

In the daytime, I pretended to be Jolie Blonde and imaged the nearby alligator basking in the sun was a green scaled dragon. I fled to the neighbor's house high up on piers to escape the yawning jaws of the massive beast. The dark, wet earth under the house became a dank, moldy dungeon. My bowl of *couche couche** became porridge instead.

At night my mama read to me---stories of a candy house far back in the woods where a witch lived.

In the daytime, I fancied that my family's houseboat was a gingerbread house decorated with candy. My houseboat was small, but it was far better than a dungeon. I did not venture far into the woods or up to a stranger's house because a witch might lurk there.

At night my mama read to me---stories of pirates seeking treasure in the bayous near our houseboat.

In the daytime I scoured the edges of our woods for pirate's treasure. I pretended that acorns were nuggets of gold. The candy whistle Papa brought me later was better than anything made of gold.

I was out on PawPaw's shrimp boat when the book lady brought more stories. I imagined that she was a lovely fairy godmother with a magical wand. One wave of the wand and she left these treasures at our door.

At night my mama read to me---stories of wishing wells and a talking fish that granted wishes. Stories of ugly ducklings and uglier trolls. She read about *Les Trois Cochons** who could talk and dance and sing.

In the daytime I followed my pet hen around the yard. I pretended she would become a beautiful swan and lay a golden egg. She did neither.

At night my mama read to me---stories of a brave tin soldier, explorers landing upon the shore of a sandy beach, and an Indian maiden yearning for her young brave away at war.

In the daytime, links of Spanish moss quivered in the sultry heat. A strand wafted down onto my lap. Fingering the piece gently, it became much more than fabric used to make bed tick. It became the beard of a Spanish explorer and the graying hair of the ghostly Indian girl still grieving for her gallant warrior gone to war.

At night my mama read to me---stories about a little girl named *Petit Rouge** and a *d'loup garou**; about a boy named Jacques* who climbed a beanstalk.

In the daytime, I climbed a wisteria vine in hopes of finding a giant with a singing harp and a chest of jewels.

I was playing along the edge of the bayou, knee-deep in cattails with Sadie when the book lady brought more stories.

As I sat at my mama's knee that night and listened in rapt attention to these stories, I envisioned the book lady to be the Indian maiden rowing over the swamp and leaving her treasures at each houseboat as she drifted past.

That night my mama read to me---stories about swamp angels and Irish moors and medieval forest.

In the daytime I fancied that the leafy curtain of a weeping willow tree was a medieval forest come to life. Swamp angels lurked in the recesses of the marsh. The grassy knolls in the distance were Irish moors where the little people dwelt.

The book lady brought us more stories today. I was home to meet her. She did not arrive in a horse-drawn carriage or on a magic carpet. Her transportation was not a white stallion or a fairy's dragonfly.

She arrived on a flat boat. Her wand was a long pole used to guide the flat boat along the bayou's watery trails.

She was neither princess nor queen, neither fairy godmother nor drifting Indian maiden.

She was short and dressed in a brown skirt and beige blouse. She wore sensible brown shoes. Her hair was cropped short and brown like mine.

Her smile was warm and friendly. Her eyes were cheery. They were filled with knowledge of secret places, fanciful adventures, and magical kingdoms.

And in her hands she held a treasure.

Artwork by: Theodore Schluenderfritz

Glossary:
* Jolie Blonde — Goldilocks
* couche couche — cornbread and milk
* Les Trois Cochons — Three Little Pigs
* Petit Rouge — Little Red Riding Hood
* d'loup garou — Cajun werewolf
* Jacque —Jack and the Beanstalk

This is dedicated to all librarians, especially the W.P.A. library workers who faced the elements and hardships of crossing over the back road hollers of the Appalachian Mountains and through the trepid swamps of Louisiana during the Great Depression to equip the American people with literature in order to educate them, to administer to them, and to build a better tomorrow for their families.

My Experience

As this book goes to print, my oldest baby is turning twenty. Twenty. What a nice rounded number. What a track record. What a wonderful life of memories and emotions and crayon pictures and spilt glasses of milk and bouquets of pretty weeds and pocketfuls of curious things, not to mention little red wagons full of picture books.

In the early years of my parenting, my first born had a steady diet of playtime at the babysitter's in the morning, *Sesame Street* after nap time, and endless readings of *Happy Birthday, Cookie Monster* during afternoons of potty training. Some Dr. Seuss was echoed in the bedroom for extra measure. This rounded off his early literary diet.

Sad, isn't it?

It's sad that as a voracious reader I, the parent and first educator of my children, didn't know anything about the fount of picture books available to me. Honestly, I had all but forgotten about them and I don't remember anyone mentioning that I should read them to my children.

> When I was a child,
> I used to speak like a child,
> think like a child,
> reason like a child;
> when I became a man,
> I did away with childish things.
> ---(1 Corinthians 13:11 *New American Standard Bible*)

First grade was a tender time warp for me of living in Dick and Jane's backyard and playing with Sally, Puff, and Spot. Starting in second grade I was exposed to chapter books which my teacher read and I enjoyed. I moved on to bigger works and along the literary highway forgot about the slender volumes from early childhood: *Millions of Cats* by Wanda Gag, *The Five Chinese Brothers* by Claire Huchet Bishop, *Rikki Tikki Tavi* by Rudyard Kipling, *Tikki Tikki Tembo* by Arlene Mosel, *The Little Prince* by Antoine de Saint-Exupéry, and *Blueberries for Sal* by Robert McCloskey.

Where had these marvelous, imaginative books gone? Nowhere, actually. Most of them were still at my local public library as were new, lively, colorful books that had begun being published at the time I embarked on my mothering career.

Once my third child came along I was knee-deep in work, carpools, Pop-tarts, class fieldtrips, and diapers. We were still reading *Happy Birthday, Cookie Monster*. I didn't have time for much else. Our life was a shuffle board and we were the disks being thrust down the lane as fast as the forces behind us pushed. On my oldest son's fifth birthday, a neighbor gave him the quirky new book *If You Give a Moose a Muffin* written by Laura Joffe Numeroff and illustrated with charming fun by Felicia Bond. Our funny bones were tickled and we were charmed---by a moose, of all things.

In the game of life, I did not realize that the forests of books jammed upon our shelves would soon prove to be a safe orchard, a protected training ground, for the little hearts entrusted to me.

With my fourth child I couldn't do it anymore. I was not the mother I wanted to be or the mother my children needed me to be. I quit work and the children and I began making the weekly story hour at the library. It was freeing! The library was free...and air-conditioned. As I sat holding my newest infant on my lap, I observed the librarians with interest. I was transported back into a world I had forgotten and I finally had

17

time to bask in the world of children. And what a lovely world it was.

The librarians didn't read the stories in monotone voices. They acted out the stories. They talked with their hands. They changed voices, danced and sang if that's what it took to capture their little audience's attention. They interacted with the children and did arts and crafts. They didn't just read to the children; they told them a story! *They skipped over words!* True, sometimes they looked very silly and I felt other mothers around me squirm with embarrassment, but storytellers are artists who are not known for being dignified. They are known for reaching out and finger-painting on a child's heart.

They slow down and paint our child's heart with their palettes and brushes because it's their job. Childhood is a time of wonder, a time for joy, and such a lovely piece of art. Educators do not have a trademark on this form of expression. Parents need to slow down and reach into their child's heart because it is our mission. No children's artist and mother teaches this better than the remarkable Tasha Tudor.

It was during this time that I realized how far I had gone in letting others do for my child what I should have been doing. I had not gone to college for education. My degree was practical and no nonsense---data processing. I now found myself full of nonsense. I devoured picture books like candy. I realized that sharing the reading experience was an art, not a science. I realized I didn't have to sit in the miniature round-robin chair and feel inferior to the teacher or librarian. I didn't have to believe that she was the only one with the education, the experience, and the tools to guide and mentor my children. I already had ten years of early childhood experience and the education and tools were just around the

18

block at the local library. Books were for all of us and there was no better way to reach out to my small children than to read to them.

During this time, a friend shared with me that we were living in a "renaissance (rebirth) of children's literature" and she encouraged me to look closer at what was being inked out in literary circles and what I was writing onto my children's heart and soul. The idea of a "renaissance of children's literature" struck a maternal cord within my heart. The tone of this message vibrated and promised the same delight and joys that came with each new child. A rebirth. A renewal of life. A renaissance of beauty. Thus began my passionate search for a complete literary education to share with my children. Rather than head back into a classroom, I headed straight to the library of great literary minds to harvest the fruit then back to my home to peel the skins off the pages, pluck out the words, squeeze the juice out of them, and then stir the sweetness and wisdom together and offer it to my children.

As though I had walked into a fairy tale, I was enchanted and began to look at picture books with a more discerning eye. I dug up old picture books from my childhood and found new ones that my children asked me to read over and over again. My friend Kimberly introduced me to the *Five in a Row* manuals by Jane Claire Lambert (http://www.fiarhq.com/). Finally, someone had developed a guide that was parent-friendly, gentle, encouraging, and full of learning possibilities. My young children and I spent a couple of years just reading, discussing, and playing with those books. We fancied around in the world of picture art and made numerous lapbooks* (ie: scrap booking for children) based on these stories. Then I began sharing picture books with my older children that had more mature messages. I did countless literature studies with my children using these

19

books. And I fell in love with an art form I didn't know existed. The books and our experiences stacked higher than the Library of Alexandria.

Ten years later I found myself moderating two online literature discussion groups, speaking and advocating for literacy, and working as a children's literature consultant and book reviewer. I wrote a literary companion book and two literature guidebooks and became a literature editor for a quarterly magazine. For the past ten years, I have allowed picture books to be a constant staple in my home. We have not been disappointed.

* For information concerning **lapbooks**, go to:

- Lapbooking Support Group:
  http://groups.yahoo.com/group/Lapbooking/

Books with great booklists to absorb:

- *Honey for a Child's Heart* by Gladys Hunt
- *Books Children Love* by Elizabeth Wilson
- *Bequest of Wings* by Annis Duff
- *Five in a Row* by Jane Claire Lambert (www.fiarhq.com)
- *Under the Chinaberry Tree* by Ann Ruethling/ Patti Pitcher (www.chinaberry.com)
- *Peak with Books* by Marjorie Nelsen/ Jan Nelsen-Parish
- *Real Learning* by Elizabeth Foss
- *The Read-Aloud Handbook* by Jim Trelease
- *Reading Magic* by Mem Fox (www.memfox.com)
- *How to Get Your Child to Love Reading* by Esme Raji Codell (www.planetesme.com)

THE HOLLY TREE.

Building Children Up

Some of you may be familiar with the little fable about the frogs hiking through a jungle's deep recesses. Suddenly the ground collapses beneath two of the frogs. The other frogs, only steps behind, jump back in fright. They observe the unlucky amphibians at the bottom of a deep dark pit, probably dug by a local native tribe. Circling the pit, they assess the situation. They inform the two unfortunate frogs that their fate is sealed. The pit is too deep to escape; they are as good as dead.

Frogs have one thing in common with human beings. God has bestowed all His creatures with the will to live. The intent to survive is so strong that both frogs ignore their companions and begin jumping mightily to escape. Their friends urge them to give up the fight and stop trying. They are goners, so why even try.

One of the frogs finally listens to the constant verbal barrage, falls with despair into a corner of the pit, and dies. The other frog continues to puff up his chest and jump with all his might. He struggles to get out. The frogs above continue to tell him to stop torturing himself and just lie down and die so as to be out of his misery. The frog does not regard their rebukes but only jumps higher and digs his webbed feet into the warm dirt until he finally makes it to the top of the hole.

Safely on the jungle floor with the other frogs, he is questioned about his bravery and perseverance in the face of a disastrous fall. At first he does not answer, but looks at them pleasantly, though baffled. Finally one of the frogs gets in his face and says, "Don't you hear us, frog? Why did you keep jumping?"

The frog signals that he is deaf and cannot hear them. The whole time he was jumping, he thought the other frogs were encouraging him to jump out of the pit.

Parents:
We are all invested in the work of building up the souls, minds, and hearts of our children and, in this process, building up personal relationships with them. Children learn on the playground that the old saying, "Sticks and stones may break my bones, but words can never hurt me." is not true after all.

Words can build up or they can tear down. Let us build-up those tender young souls because, if we do not do it, no one else will.

Relationships and Connections

Edmund Gosse wrote in *Father and Son*, "Never, in all my early childhood, did anyone address to me the affecting preamble: 'Once upon a time!'... I can but think that my parents were in error thus to exclude the imaginary from my outlook upon facts. They desired to make me truthful; the tendency was to make me positive and skeptical. Had they wrapped me in the soft folds of supernatural fancy, my mind might have been longer content to follow their traditions in an unquestioning spirit."

This quote gives the parent pause. Can reading to a child teach the child countless lessons in life without the parent having to preach and lecture? Can reading to a child help him to discern truths and fallacies? Can reading to a child overshadow any parenting failures and misguided discipline? Can reading to a child build a family culture far beyond the hearth?

A wise man once said that children are the message we leave to a world we will not see. What message do you want to leave your child and, in doing so, a world you will not see? If this was your last day on earth, what words would you leave behind for your child? Picture books can carry powerful, lasting messages.

Children's literature is so much more than sweet idealism and romantic grandeur. It is a wonderful orchard where sharing is encouraged. You can show your child what interests you and cultivate these interests in them. You can give them a lesson in morality and virtue without sounding preachy and opinionated. The ground of youth is rich and fertile. Stories endure within the soul as well as in the mind.

The written word is doubly valuable because it is engraved for all to see and read. It can be pondered over twice as long as a spoken word. And there is no denying that it was ever said. The word is there and it is a powerful admonition towards good or evil. It builds our concept of what is good and what is evil and challenges us. The time with your child that this book promotes and the picture books it suggests you use during this time frame are mere stepping stones towards empowering your children with a positive view of the wonderful world in which we live and their place in it.

All can benefit from a visit to this land of "once upon a time", to this land of milk and honey. Tasting the milk of human kindness and the honey of "happily ever after" that is found in these quaint tales can revitalize us and give us all renewed hope. Sometimes we realize that our dreams weren't as impossible as we thought, had we only kept reaching—and reading. After all, reaching for a high ideal is better than falling down into the pit without ever trying.

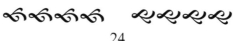

The Best-Kept Secret in American Education

We really must rethink the way we think of storybooks as learning tools. They are treasures. They are works of art. They are gateways and portals that open up a whole new world for you and your child. This world can be enjoyed at the age of five, at the age of fifteen, and at the age of fifty. The idea, as one mother wrote, that "Too many parents think that the beginning of schooling should mean the end of picture books," needs to be abandoned.

We must focus on a daily environment of weaving books with life. As children's author Melissa Wiley (the *Little House Martha* and *Charlotte series*) ended her 2003 NACHE convention talk (www.nache.com) entitled *Literature in All its Beauty and Form*: "I strew the path and I open the door to conversation. And we have books for breakfast, literature for lunch, Tennyson for tea, Dickens for dessert, a Midsummer Night's Dream for a midafternoon snack. We enjoy daily feasts of living books." ~ Melissa Wiley

There are so many nourishing, delicious books out there. Today's picture books are refreshingly vibrant and visual, blown-up, over-sized, and paint a masterfully lasting

25

impression. Expose your children by putting these big-screen classics 'in their face' and enjoying them together...over popcorn.

In his book *The Read Aloud Handbook*, Mr. Trelease writes on page xii-xiii:

"...all anyone needs --- is a free public library card and the determination to invest her mind and time in her child's future. The investment can be as small as fifteen minutes a day."

"Extensive research has proven that reading aloud to a child is the single most important factor in raising a reader. *These inexpensive fifteen minutes a day are the best-kept secret in American education.*" (emphasis my own)
(Trelease, 2001, page. xii-xiii, *The Read-Aloud Handbook*)

When I read these words by Jim Trelease, the American guru on the art of reading aloud, I was fascinated, inspired, and held bound.

Fifteen minutes a day! Could sparking a love for learning really be that simple? Could a mere fifteen minutes a day be that powerful? Could a simple fifteen minutes a day release parents and caretakers of the guilt of not empowering our children, of not spending time with them, of not slowing down?

I thought about this quote a lot; and I thought about it some more. I read what Jim Trelease had to say about this secret fifteen minutes of read-aloud time that can promote readers and, thus, lifelong learners and I came to some obvious and not-so-obvious conclusions.

First, I embraced the idea that this precious fifteen minutes of time shared each day between a parent and child could benefit the child's intellectual, mental, and physical needs. Secondly, I discerned that if these fifteen minutes could touch the child's intellectual, mental, and physical sides then it could benefit his spiritual being as well the emotional being. Thirdly, I realized how these mere fifteen minutes a day could embrace and explore the artistic aspect which the educational system is at risk of abandoning yet which is essential to man as a creative, spiritual, vital being. Fourthly, I knew in my heart that no parent in this crazy-busy, over-taxed, over-committed world of ours could deny their child a mere fifteen-minutes a day. Lastly, I could not fail to realize the intimate connection between this "inexpensive fifteen minutes a day" and the time it takes to read a children's picture book. So I embroidered the quote and the mindset onto my sleeve and began to research and practice it on my children.

Excerpts (where noted) are used from *The Read-Aloud Handbook* by Jim Trelease, Copyright © Jim Trelease, Fifth Edition, 2001, Penguin Books (http://www.trelease-on-reading.com/)

Cultivating the Imagination

Reading and studying picture books, while using hands-on lesson play with them in the company of our children, gives our brains and, thus our imagination, an invigorating massage.

Helen Keller realized the importance of the imagination and the ability that separates human beings from all other living creatures---the ability to think. She writes: "The most beautiful world is always entered through imagination." (Helen Keller, 1908)

Writers today know how important it is to stimulate the minds of our youth. Charley Reese writes: "Let's hope...that parents will continue to encourage their children to read because reading is far more important than playing computer games or going to the movies. Neither of those media works the brain and stimulates the imagination, and imagination is a key ingredient of thinking. Most of the real scientific breakthroughs resulted from imagination. Only after something new is visualized can reason and experiment be employed to bring it into reality." (*Nothing Stimulates Imagination like Good Literature,* by Charley Reese, July 2007, King Feature Syndicate)

Is imagination important in today's technological world? You better believe it is. It's invaluable and at risk for extinction if we don't allow our children time to be children and time to just be. Time even to be bored. Time to let one's thoughts soar. Time to just think and wonder and create. Time to let their imagination take over. Does that surprise you?

I can't think of any place more boring than a jail cell but that is exactly where some of the greatest trains of thought have been derailed and refueled. Dante created *The Inferno* while in jail. John Bunyan wrote *The Pilgrim's Progress* while in jail. And, of course, we have the example of Cervantes and Don Quixote. While in jail their minds were the only part that could be unleashed and sent soaring. They left behind their *magnum opus* (great work) for future generations to meditate on and decipher. The Broadway musical *Man of LaMancha* is set in a dungeon and gives a passionate plea for the preservation of beauty, romance, faith, and (yes, even) the power of idealistic imagination. Imagination is what takes us out of ourselves when this world becomes unbearable and lonely or we become disillusioned over lost childhood days.

In the world of literature, imagination has gifted us with Lewis' *Narnia*, Tolkien's *Lord of the Rings* trilogy, numerous fairy tales, *The Wizard of Oz, Alice in Wonderland,* and other countless treasures. Walt Disney almost single-handedly became the catalyst for taking literature and, with a wave and a click of his camera, transporting us into a magical adventure. Sure, the Brothers Grimm and Hans Christian Andersen may very well be turning over in their graves; but no one can deny that Walt Disney's Wonderful World has taken countless hearts and brought literature alive to many. Whether you love or hate these imaginative works of fiction, think for a moment what would the world be without magical tea cups and Mad Hatter un-birthdays. What if we had never heard the words "There's no place like home," from a little girl in Kansas who truly knew where her heart lay? What if we hadn't wandered through the jungles with Mowgli and the author who imagined him, Rudyard Kipling; and Hugh Lofting's Puddleby-on-the-Marsh with his character Dr. Dolittle and his scads of animal friends?

Look what the gift of imagination has bestowed on the world at large as inspired by someone else's imagination.

Things that we can hardly envision living without: telephones, televisions, computers, etc., are things that came about because someone had a vision, someone else had the innovation, someone else had the knowledge, and still another had the finances. Without the gift of imagination and innovation, we would still be living in caves and drawing in the dirt.

 Picture-Perfect Photo Tip

"The imagination is the bridge between the heart and mind." ~ Michael Card

"Imagination is more important than knowledge. For knowledge is limited to all we now know and understand, while imagination embraces the entire world, and all there ever will be to know and understand." ~ Albert Einstein

To Reach the Impossible Dream

As we grow older, this world becomes intangible and impalpable. We are not connected with it as closely as our children are. The reality and harshness betrays the calm, velvety days of our youth. As adults, life tells us that books are the illusion; we live the reality. Illusion resides in the inner recesses of our mind and soul. It is not in the world around us and often does not resemble it.

We are like the deaf frog in the pit. We see those people looking at us through the cultural lens of society. They are telling us that the chivalry and spiritual quest found in books is all an illusion and cannot be obtained in real life because it is not real. An unread person might believe this fallacy. Without the divine guidance that is received and sustained from reading, they fall back into the pit to wilt from the difficulties and harshness of real life. We might be deaf but we are not blind to the fact that the real world is not always gallant and spiritually substantial. We know that some say reading is an escape from the world. We wonder what is out there to nourish and build up the hearts, minds and souls of our children. We know that books give us an ideal that probably won't be found on this earth, but we prefer to turn a deaf ear to the masses and keep jumping higher for that unreachable dream that was so evasive to the main character in the play, *Man of LaMancha*.

The *Man of LaMancha* takes place in a dungeon during the Inquisition. An abstract poet/playwright is left to confront a den of prisoners who are all too aware of the falsehoods and harshness of life. They are the playwright's harshest critics. It is up to him to convince them, through his play, that life is what you make of it. At death's door, you must have touched the sweetness of milk and honey; if not in the real sense, then

31

in the abstract sense. Otherwise, life has no meaning or sweetness.

The Man of LaMancha shows that real literature is much more than just words on a page. The prisoners realize that what the old man holds dear in this rat-infested dungeon are the pages in his hands. With illiterate contempt, they confiscate his manuscript and threaten to destroy it. But the old playwright has vision and insight beyond the pages of his manuscript, beyond the dinginess of the dungeon and beyond the ignorance of his fellow prison mates. His words take on a life of their own. The characters he creates with his words live and breathe. They affect the souls of many.

The play ends as the old man goes to trial. He leaves behind a dungeon full of prisoners singing *The Impossible Dream.* The old man has restored to them visions of higher aspirations. He has given them the knowledge that there is no shame in being thought a fool for love and art. The only wrong with being in a pit is in not reaching ever higher.

The unreachable dreams that we so often find in great books are the very dreams that give our life meaning and joy as children. This land of milk and honey becomes that bigger image, that richer treasure, that Promised Land because it was what we held near and dear to us. It is a gift given to us by the divine hand of God. It is a gift which enlightens our hearts and souls even as adults. These dreams and books are not just fanciful images and unobtainable thoughts. They are there for a reason. They are thoughts and words that are put on paper to build us up and make us stronger than we are.

With children's literature the honey is even sweeter. While young, the child is given a safe emotional lifeline. When older, he has an escape route stored in his mind to pull him safely up to that unreachable star...a heavenly cause...an impossible dream.

Children's literature offers the adult an invitation to step through a magical wardrobe of past dreams and lost desires. Once again we can savor fanciful images and regain a sense of self and a passion for life. Children's literature gives us grassroots to grab onto and pull ourselves out of the pit of despair.

Quote: "There is nothing like a dream to create the future." ~ Victor Hugo

Assignment for Parents: Check with your local bookstore or library or go here http://www.herbleonhard.com/books/Billy's-Mountain.pdf for a copy of *Billy's Mountain* by author Steve Richardson and illustrator Herb Leonhard. Read this with your child and ask him what his dreams are. Are they ordinary? Or *extra-ordinary*?

A Word about Reading

I cringe when people make comments about people who love reading: "He lives in his own little world." "She lives inside the pages of a book." "They live within a make-believe world."

That's not it at all. It makes the reader sound like a disillusioned recluse on the outside of town, as though he has leprosy or something.

Literature and the reading of it is not about getting away from the world or living apart from the world or isolating oneself into a make-believe world. Literature and reading is all about *understanding* the world, *accepting* the world we live in and our place in it, *reaching* a higher chapter of being, and *helping* us make the world better than we see it outside our glass tower. It's all about turning the page and bridging the gap.

If anyone still doubts this theory, go see a performance of *Man of La Mancha*. Cervantes' idealism is also mocked...and nobly defended.

A very dear girl in my life loves to read. She also lives in a very dysfunctional family with little time to herself. There is never enough money. There is a drinking problem in the house and lots of arguing. So she reads. Yes, while she's reading it allows her some "my space" and peace and takes her outside of her surroundings, if only for a little while; but the real treasure and fruit in reading is that by being introduced to a variety of characters (good and bad) and circumstances (good and bad) and situations (good and bad) and events (good and bad), she walks away from those books equipped...hopefully...to handle real life.

Those books show her in a more positive light reasons why people do what they do. Those books teach her to understand why people react the way they react; and, most importantly, those books help her to realize that nothing that has happened in her life thus far is through any fault of hers. Those books teach her to understand how and why things happen and to, hopefully, prevent her from making the same mistakes. In short, books broaden our view of the world around us.

It's not at all about living in another world. It's all about dealing with the world in which we live and making it a better place if we can. Sometimes it only allows life to be more bearable.

Books are the bait that hooks the fish. They are not what the fish lives on. Books add spice to our lives and they nourish us, but they are not the meat that sustains us through job losses, divorces, deaths, etc. Books are a reflection of ourselves; they are not the flesh and blood on the other side of the bathroom countertop.

Still books are quite real and, indeed, have a life of their own. Reading is---in reality---having a conversation with another person. They talk. You listen and, sometimes, debate the material in your own mind. Reading allows us to see and hear what's in another person's brain. It allows us to feel their emotions. Books are really the first virtual reality that ever existed, instead of the one-sided view you see on television, books give you a three-dimensional (even a five-dimensional) viewing. Front row seat, if you ask me.

Please remember this when you see your child sitting a corner reading. Don't view him as being lazy, self-centered, isolated, or one-dimensional. At that moment he is so much more than that. He is centering in on the whole force of the universe. He is solving all the problems in the world. He is exploring lands outside the living room window. He is wandering the streets of London as an orphan and learning the tricks of survival in the wild with an Indian friend. He is roping steers on the high prairie and sailing with pirates to find a lost treasure. And he is equipping himself with armor to battle dragons, save damsels in distress, map his way through Middle-earth, and scale Mount Olympus. Your child is not escaping the world when reading. Quite the opposite. He is equipping himself with tools to go out and meet it.

Why not join him? Ask him what he's reading. Ask him to share parts of it with you. Listen attentively. Ask him about the characters, the plot, the setting. Nineteenth-century teacher Charlotte Mason knew what she was writing about when she advocated narration within the home and the school.

Without books we cannot meet famous minds and speakers. Without books we cannot understand the abstract things of life like morals and virtues and vices. Without books we lack self-expression. Without books we forget where we came from. Without books the past becomes as dry and lost as the sand that blows across the Egyptian desert. Without books we become speechless.

Picture-Perfect Photo Tip

Open a family photo album and tell me there is no story written upon the pages. If you can't remember the story, give the album to your children and let them read it to you.

Why Use Picture Books?

At a young age I remember wondering how older people could read books without pictures. The very thought was unthinkable. Even today I love the visual imagery sprinkled in books like little nosegays strewn around a storybook garden. As I grew up, I began to enjoy the *Little House* books and walked along many fanciful trails with *Anne of Green Gables*. I waltzed through summer with *Gone with the Wind*. I adored *Five Little Peppers and How They Grew*. These books have lasted and still have a special place upon my bookshelves, but the picture books were the gateway---the portals---the ascension to greater things, to greater exposure, to greater works. Without picture books, books as a whole part of my learning and growing experience would never have held such special appeal and purpose for me. I also discovered (and rediscovered) wisdom, inspiration, and beauty in the picture books of my youth. How you ask?

Picture books are no longer just for little kids. A whole art form and emergence of learning is stemming from this new era of great picture books. Picture books are a surprising art

37

form in and of themselves. Some are masterpieces. Some are merely joyful reminders of forgotten childhood days. They are treasures that attempt to bring beauty and escape to an ever increasingly difficult and quickening world around us. Parents and educators can, and have, made them so much more than paper products anchored on shelves with dust collecting upon the spine.

Walt Disney knew the truth. He is quoted, "There is more treasure in books than in all the pirate's loot on Treasure Island."

Books are not a boring fabrication of life. We need to look for ways to blend them into our life and daily activities. If you take a trip to the beach, pick up several beach books to read beforehand. If you're practicing for a sporting event, read several Olympic books and other sports literature. If your family is looking into adopting a child, there are some excellent illustrated books available on adoption. Make a timeline of every major war and select great picture books about that war. Mark it on your timeline as you read the book.

Picture books, like small children, aren't given enough credit. I share this information because I am passionately delighted by picture books myself. I share this information because I have teenage children with whom I share these books. I share this information because of the freedom I have found in the information offered in Jim Trelease's *The Read-Aloud Handbook* which supports these books for all ages. I share this information because I have heard of teachers sharing these books with older students in the classroom. I share this information because I have read and heard that authors and illustrators of these books feel it is their vocation and their mission to share an art form in their books. One of the primary goals of this book is to expose your children, and yourself, to various authors and artists who have made it their mission and vocation to bring their talent into the world of youth. They are on a quest to make childhood more meaningful and beautiful and richer, and educational, than it ever was before. Through this book and their talents, you will be introduced to the best that children's publishing has to offer today.

Your child may become a teenager who thinks storybooks are silly, but only if they weren't read to him as a child. Picture books take only fifteen-minutes a day. I can guarantee that when he has his own child, he'll remember...he'll remember the books you read to him and the fifteen-minutes you spent with him. This is doable for every schooling parent, every working parent, every traveling parent, every reluctant reader, and every struggling reader.

You will make memories that will last forever. These memories will certainly last much longer than fifteen-minutes a day. I guarantee it.

In Defense of Picture Books

Some parents and educators believe that picture books are what nineteenth-century English educator Charlotte Mason was speaking of when she mentioned *twaddle*. They see picture books as something the child needs to be weaned from. Yet nothing could be further from the true image. Picture books are not twaddle...not even for the adult let alone the child. Many parents and older children find great delight in sharing a childhood storybook favorite with their children.

One mother admits: "As an adult I also enjoy the beauty and lovely style of picture books without feeling that my children are the only ones that can get pleasure out of them." Another parent noticed how picture books are the bridge to chapter books. They are very necessary for young children and not at all bad for older readers to reread and enjoy. This parent, Kelly Gibbons, wrote: "Charlotte Mason advocated the use of beautiful illustrations. True, most of those were great works of art. However, even today, some children's books are beautifully illustrated. To sum up, I think there are a time and a place for picture books in the lives of children. It is a necessary stepping stone. Without picture books the

'Internet Generation' may not develop an interest in or a life-long affection for books."

Julie in Washington offers, "There are LOTS of opportunities to discuss art techniques (while using picture books). Books printed in recent years often describe the artwork medium (watercolor or such) and expertise on the copyright page. And there is high quality poetry and prose published in picture books too. I think that quality picture books will build a solid foundation for later appreciation of quality literature AND art! Don't be in a hurry to give them up!"

So don't wean your children too early from the bounty of picture books that exist today. A beautiful picture book a day can give your child a new lease on reading. After you've read the very best, the most elite picture books, you begin to see the difference and so will your child. Treat yourself and indulge in these books alongside of your young children and your teenagers alike. Teenagers, as well as elderly people, remember and treasure special picture books throughout their life. These budding adults can share their favorite picture books with a younger sibling, cousin, niece, or nephew. Upon finding a favorite picture book, it is common to feel a peaceful, tranquil comfort settle into our heart and soul. Don't give that up too soon.

Picture-Perfect Photo Tip
"What the soul cries out for is the resurrection of the senses."
~ C.S. Lewis

Struggling with Read-Alouds

"But I struggle with reading aloud and my husband never reads to the children."

What do you do when the art of reading aloud to your children does not come naturally or easily to you? Perhaps there are dishes to wash, leftover supper to put away, school work to check, and soccer practices to attend. Or maybe you have a high energy non-reader who cannot sit through anything longer than a Dr. Seuss book without playing Peter Pan on the living room furniture. Perhaps you are just starting to embrace a literary lifestyle in your family and your children are not sure how to behave during read aloud time.

Jim Trelease reminds us on page 101 of *The Read-Aloud Handbook*: "Remember that reading aloud comes naturally to VERY FEW people. To do it successfully and with ease you must practice."

When a child reads a book or has a book read to him:

1. He uses his own imagination which, to quote Albert Einstein: "… is more important than knowledge."
2. He uses his brain to *think*. His brain has to visualize, to observe, to contemplate, and to analyze on its own power. On a television screen, someone else is doing all these things for him.
3. There is a human bonding there, a fellowship, a joining of souls in the one reading and the one being read to.

Regarding the bonding issue, let me share this quote from *Inside Picture Books* by Ellen Handler Spitz: "We care, and we take care, to know a great deal about what goes into our children's bodies; we need to be no less attentive to what goes

42

into their minds." She goes further to write: "Picture books, unlike television and the other electronic media ubiquitously available today, require the participation of warm, breathing adult human partners who have available laps, keen eyes and ears, arms adept at holding while turning pages, and perhaps a flair for the dramatic."

If, as someone wise once said, "Reading is culture," we need to be the troubadours who sing poetic stories to our children so that they in turn will sing the same lullabies to their children and these living messages will not die but flourish in the hearts and souls of a new generation.

I want to share a couple of personal experiences of parents who struggled with read-alouds and overcame the illusion of monsters in the closet.

My friend Michelle Grunkemeyer shared her experience as she tried and succeeded in welcoming books into their home and embracing family read-alouds:

"I have struggled with reading aloud to my kids. I am a voracious reader but hate reading aloud. I started last year with a booklist for first grade but other than the *Homer Price* books, my kids were less than inspired. They never brought me the books to read and didn't want to sit and listen. We have started and never finished *Mountain Born, Wheel on the School, Minn of the Mississippi, Charlotte's Web* and more because they just never got into the storyline or wanted to finish them. We had a wonderful breakthrough this year. I attended a WholeHearted Child workshop by Sally Clarkson (www.wholeheart.org) where I received permission to move back to picture books. For the past month, I've been checking out books from the library - Caldecott winners primarily. My kids are now hooked! They clamor for me to read to them and we've found some really beautiful books. My oldest is in

43

second grade and struggles with reading but he's taking books upstairs to look at (not read but at least he's opening them). This past week was the first time I checked out a book on tape, *Wind in the Willows*. My children are learning to listen and narrate back to me what's happened and they are enjoying the book. I also am reading a book that has seriously re-inspired me in regards to reading aloud...Jim Trelease's *The Read Aloud Handbook*. It does have a reading list in the back but what was unique for me was his argument for the necessity and benefit of reading aloud to all ages of children. He talks about how older kids in schools love to be read to and how so much is passed on to our children by reading aloud to them. The stories he relates about how reading aloud has touched children's lives is inspiring." ~ Michelle Grunkemeyer

* * * * *

My friend Linda Dalton shares here about her struggles with reading aloud to her very active boys:

"If I can do it, *anyone* can! Believe me! We have six children. The boys were born pretty close to one another. I started reading to them as newborns as I had done with my daughter. I was expecting the same reaction I received with my firstborn, which was sitting still gazing at the picture books, Ha! That is the *last* thing both of my boys did. They couldn't wait to get out of my lap. It didn't take long before I gave in and let them loose.

"I thought, well I could read to them as they play. Ha!! I was insulted even more. Not only did they play, they talked and giggled with each other as I read. I remember actually reading lines into the books like "Why am I reading this? Nobody is listening or even cares?" They kept on playing didn't give me the time of day. I kept reading and reading.

44

Feeling completely ignored I persisted still. Grant it, the boys were still very young but my daughter by this age was sitting through twenty books easily and wanted more! I couldn't even get my boys to listen to one!

"I realized I had to keep it simple for my own sanity. I was not a reader as a child or even as an adult up to that point. I thought I would faint if I even attempted to read great books to my kids if I couldn't even sit there through them myself. *My* attention span on books was itty bitty too!

I began to evaluate and shape-up my criteria to get us all reading:

- We needed a huge access for reading…the library
- We wanted books with character
- To hold my children's attention, books would be no longer than 2-3 lines per page
- We would use booklists that were available to us

"I started at the library with the letter A in juvenile! We went to the library once a week, if we are fortunate twice. We would start at A and get all the books that would fit my criteria. What happened when we got to Z? Start all over. By doing so, not only did we get in and out of the library but we got to all those great books on the many booklists I perused at one point or another.

"Let me tell you how this story ends. My boys now *love* books. They pour over them like butter! A number of things came about with my criterion that was made out of necessity. My kids developed a passion for books. My reading level soared from reading these simple lovely books year after year. My eldest daughter gets excited when we come across this or that book because it evokes such fond memories for her. She went on reading all those great books on her own. I tried to read them to her but her speed surpassed mine years ago. I guess I can still read them to the boys.

"So see, keep it simple and easy. It's very doable. Take it from me, one who *hated* reading or listening to books, who now has an on going love affair with them! The fruits are many." ~ Linda Dalton

The Reluctant Reader

I think reluctant readers are formed when we push them too fast. We push them to get the phonic sounds right. We push them to more grown-up fare. We push them to read text books too much. We push them to grow up too soon. In November 2003, I was in Baton Rouge, Louisiana for the annual Book Festival. A little girl who looked to be about second or third grade came over to my table and began looking through the lapbooks and notebooks I had on display. She saw my daughter's *Blueberries for Sal* lapbook, grabbed it, and said *"Oh, I love this book!"*

I encouraged her to read it again and do her own lapbook while showing her some of the things we had done using the book as suggested in the *Five in a Row Curriculum* by Jane Claire Lambert. But the little girl slowly set the lapbook down and said, "Oh, I can't read it again. My teacher said it's a baby book. Only first graders can read it."

I thought to myself, "This is a perfect example of 'death of a reader', and the schools wonder why we live in the age of non-readers."

Often we forget that it was picture books that first welcomed our children into the world of books. Our older children begin scoffing at a book and saying, "That's stupid. That's a baby book!"

Where do they get this attitude? From a teacher's prompting that the book is babyish? From our prompting that they need to find something more challenging or that the curriculum demands that they read something more challenging? Do they get this attitude because they've only watched the Disney movies versus reading the original tales? Do they get this attitude because we, as parents and teachers,

47

have read only 'twaddle' to our children instead of heartfelt, wonderful books with beautiful, rich illustrations in them?

The picture books my older children don't call babyish or stupid are the books I read to them when they were little. When a book is taken out that was read to them when they were young, it is greeted by "Oh, I remember this book!" "Gosh, I loved that book!"

So I encourage you, if you have a reluctant reader, please don't put those picture books away. Do just the opposite. Take them off the shelf and read them…together. Jim Trelease reminds us on page 100 of *The Read-Aloud Handbook*:

"Picture books can be read easily to a family of children widely separated in age. Novels, however, pose a challenge."

Notice, he doesn't say a threat or impossibility…just a challenge. So start small. A chapter book can be overwhelming to a beginning reader, a reluctant reader, and their parents. Start small with picture books.

I want to offer you something to keep the guilt at bay, to keep the enthusiasm for reading up, something to inspire you and your children towards reading the longer books.

Here is my friend Linda's personal experience with struggling through read-louds, struggling with a reluctant reader, and her own personal success story as she evolved from a fidgety, restless fiesta of energy (she's still a fidgety, restless fiesta of energy) into an avid, passionate reader all with the help of picture books:

"If you have a reluctant reader in your home, take heart. We're not that way forever! Some of us bloom later than others. Just keep plugging away. It will pay off. Keep reading yourself. Turn off the TV. It robs you and your family of more than we realize.

"I did not read as a child. I didn't have parents who were readers either. As I grew, so did my homework in school. I read what I had to and couldn't recollect anything past the quiz that followed.

"A couple of years ago my husband asked me when had I become an avid reader. He knew he hadn't married one! It dawned on me that it had happened unexpectedly. When our eldest daughter was born I set this rule about which books to pick-up from the library. It could be no more than two lines per page, something beautiful to look at, and not anything that would be against our faith. I selected books under this 'rule' from the time she was eight weeks old and have continued doing it with our other children. What happened in this interim was unexpected considering I was reading to her for *her* sake and not mine. Because I had stayed with this level of books on a regular basis for so many years my reading ability and interests in books soared. I looked forward to what was in store in the next book just as my daughter did.

"As time went on I found myself reading my own books every chance I got. You would have never known that I was not a *reader* as a child. I just had to find something that motivated me and staying at a level that literally hurled me into a level I had always admired about others but actually found out-of-reach for myself because I wasn't *that* kind of child.

"The most important tidbit I have discovered for my family is that there is not replacement for *real* books. My daughter has learned more from real books, per se, than any text book I could have ever handed her. Her knowledge goes to depths that my husband and I vaguely remember from our college days. Stories have something a child can hang onto. My daughter's knowledge has been like a patchwork quilt that she has pieced together. There is not order, just pleasure, and beauty.

"Let me tell you, it is gorgeous because it is filled with love. If a subject comes up (just about anything) she is like a submarine. She dives, dives, dives. She knows all these little anecdotes and long woven tales about time periods and people in history. It's nothing I have taught her. It is that incredible journey she has been on called a book.

"To all of us late bloomers...Cheers! To all you moms that bore us...Patience, it does end happily ever after!"
~ Linda Dalton

Picture-Perfect Photo Tip
"Passion is to picture books as yeast is to bread: the one is nothing without the other." ~ Mem Fox from her book *Dear Mem Fox*

The Teenage Reader

It may surprise you that I am recommending picture books for teenagers but I ask that you bear with me while I explain this concept. I don't want you to think: "Oh, no! She's going to tell me to read picture books to my teenager." I don't want you to think I'm trying to insult your intelligence or that of your child's.

There were times when I was dealing with my own teenagers that I found a picture book could better simplify things that were mournfully drawn-out and completely over the child's head in a dry text book. Sometimes a picture book made them care about a subject or a historical person whom they had not cared about before. Many times, a picture book condensed into a nutshell what I had spent the past hour trying to tell them. In history, a world and time zones that reach far and wide, I have found that a picture book can prove to be a capsule-size time machine which can be swallowed more easily than trying to climb and ride the whole elephant.

Having the older ones read illustrated books to younger siblings while in the car, at bed time, during potty training sessions, and on camping trips is great exposure. Many children can be exposed to beautiful, fun, insightful books this way.

Jim Trelease writes this about teenagers and picture books: "A good story is a good story. Beautiful and stirring pictures can move fifteen-year-olds as well as five-year-olds. A picture book(s) should be someplace on the reading list of every class at every level." (Pages 90-92 of *A Read-Aloud Handbook*, Fourth Edition) This was so freeing for me.

The Little Prince by Antoine de Saint-Exupéry has been used for translation work in a high school French class. Oscar

Wilde's *The Happy Prince* has been used for analysis. Dr. Seuss' *Oh, the Places You'll Go!* has been read to eighth graders and graduating seniors. And can anyone imagine growing up without reading Shel Silverstein's *The Giving Tree?*

Yes, picture books are acceptable and readable with teenagers; especially today's selections. It's important to locate a picture book with a message. Picture books are also great for teaching teenagers about imagery and metaphors and similes, etc. Don't listen to the high school English teacher who tells you that your child will fail the state regulated test if he doesn't read Shakespeare play texts only. Instead pick up an illustrated book on Shakespeare such as Aliki's *William Shakespeare and the Globe* and *All the World's a Stage* by Rebecca Piatt Davidson/ Anita Lobel. Read the Shakespeare plays by Bruce Coville. These books will take 15-20 minutes of your time and your teenager's time to read. Don't make him read for the sake of a test and grade. Just make him care.

Have your high-schooler read Shakespeare's plays, but don't think you have to hand him a full-blown Shakespeare play and have him read it for a report. Don't have him sit at his desk for an hour trying to decipher the text alone. That's hard work, even for an adult. It's not fair to your high schooler. It will only build resentment for Shakespeare and his stage. Use Bruce Coville's illustrated books instead and get an interest going, build a love of the storyline and plots and characters first.

After reading this with you, if your child decides to go on his own trail reading and discovering and studying Shakespeare, you have exposed him, you have planted the seed, you have invited him. Let him follow the trail wherever it leads.

List for Teenaged Readers and Reluctant Readers

☐ *The Little Prince* by Antoine de Saint-Exupéry (various illustrated versions are available)

☐ *The Treasure* by Uri Shulevitz

☐ *Sorry* by Jean Van Leeuwen/ Brad Sneed

☐ *Oh, the Places You'll Go!* by Dr. Seuss

☐ *The Tin Forest* by Helen Ward/ Wayne Anderson

☐ *Once Upon a Time* by Niki Daly

☐ *The Bee Tree* by Patricia Polacco

☐ *Thank you, Mr. Falker* by Patricia Polacco

☐ *Up the Learning Tree* by Marcia Vaughan/ Derek Blanks

☐ *Amber on the Mountain* by Tony Johnston/ Robert Duncan

☐ *Raising Sweetness* by Diane Stanley/ G. Brian Karas

☐ *More than Anything Else* by Marie Bradby/ Chris Soentpiet

Guilt-Free Reading

Do you have a great sense of guilt in finding time to read to each of your children — no matter how much you strive to do so, no matter how important you believe it to be? Recently a mother questioned the problem she was having in reading aloud to her children. I could relate. I understood her dilemma all too well. Not all of my children are natural readers. With five children we've had our share of toddlers climbing on our heads while Pippi Longstocking flips pancakes and eggs over hers, spilt drinks on the coffee table that demand instant attention while Jack the brindle bulldog is left lost on the high prairie, and background sing-a-longs that stifle out my storyteller's voice while taking us out of the story. And, yes, we've had our own issues of television and computer games taking dominance over books in the lives of my teenagers. We live in a technological world. None of us are immune.

It is not a picture-perfect world, no matter how hard we try to make our homes magical. But children *need* to be read to. Statistics show that many of the educational problems and low performances in school would be eliminated if children were read to from the cradle and beyond. For the most part, the effort is worth all the interruptions and, with time, children who have been read to *lots* during their formative years will embrace this time and grow to love it.

Why is it so important, you ask?

I could simply direct you to Jim Trelease's outstanding *The Read-Aloud Handbook* or Gladys Hunt's wonderful *Honey for a Child's Heart* but, briefly, the reason we need to read aloud to our children is to get them to *think*.

The technological age we live in with its blast of communication and blare of information has dulled our listening skills and our logical thought process. Everything we process is in a box...literally. Television and computers are wonderful resources but they give us someone else's thoughts while color-coding our own.

Books and hands-on learning take us outside the box...literally...and push us into a personal adventure devoid of wires and special effects. There are no connections. It's only us and a mentor speaking to us from the recesses of a book. There is nothing there to hold us bound and tied. There are no links there to divert our thoughts down another railroad track. Our own imagination and our own sensory experience guide us and lead us outside the boxes framed-up and programmed by others.

Where our society is lacking is not in teaching children *how to read* but in teaching them to *love and appreciate* reading. Once they have the love and appreciation, there will be no stopping them. They will only learn this through daily frequent read-alouds; and it need only take fifteen-minutes of your day.

There are so many wonderful reading selections and passionate readers want to read them all ... but we just can't. So here is where I let you all off the hook. Your job in sharing literature with your children is not to read every single book to them. There will always be books left unread.

There will always be a new bestseller being published and old classics that we just can't seem to find time to read. There is an easier way, a more freeing alternative for releasing that guilt and it still puts books and reading at the forefront of your educational plan and your desire to share them with your child. It's so easy that it's insane more parents, myself included, take so long to turn on the nightlight. It takes only a picture book and fifteen-minutes a day to reach the impossible dream of bonding relationships and forming connections.

Here's a golden opportunity! The Children's Hour!

With the encouragement and support of Jim Trelease, I am going to offer you a new concept. I call it the Children's Hour. It's very freeing and helps the parent to stay on a consistent path of reading to and with their children. It consists of reading fifteen-minutes each day to your children.

Picture-Perfect Photo Tip

"Pick one subject a year in which to become *'an expert'*. First read the easiest books you can find on the subject to get a handle on the content. For unit subjects such as in history or science, I find the easiest little kids' picture book I can on the subject to reteach myself what I've forgotten from my own schooling. I think I've learned more reading little kids' books than I ever did from textbooks!" ~ Kathy von Duyk

Picture-Perfect Photo Tip
On Daddy's Lap

I want to give you all something to think on.

You know how Dad comes home from work and the little ones say "Daddy's Home!" Dad kicks off his shoes, sits down in his big easy recliner, props his feet up and takes a long drink of iced tea, cola, or a beer. The little ones climb onto his lap. If you say "Honey, would you read this book?" he'll look at you and say one of two things, "Babe, I'm tired. I don't feel like reading." Or, "How long is it?"

We often lament over dads being more helpful in the education of our children or simply spending more time with them but, the long and short of it is that, there is really no excuse for not taking fifteen-minutes a day to make contact with your child and give them a beautiful idea, a beautiful thought to take to bed with them.

Hand a nice picture book to the child and tell him, *"Go ask Daddy to read this to you."* Dads don't often turn down their children's request...and they certainly can't (or shouldn't) turn down a simple request for a fifteen-minute connection with their child. It's all about building relationships.

CHILDREN'S HOUR*
(A Twelve Month Historical Timeline)

The Children's Hour is a twelve-month historical timeline for families. I have done my best to ensure that every illustrated book listed is the very best of vivid imagery, promising an eyeful of educational beauty, knowledge, and emotion to adults and teenagers alike with a smattering of color for preschoolers as well. My main focus was to gather a selection of historical and biographical titles and list them within a dated timeline.

The booklist averages many books per month. Read them at your own pace. While its overall focus is history, biographical-related, there are other books thrown into this selection to add enjoyment for different ages within a family during the various seasons and holidays that frame each month. I have made a special attempt to include the following subject in each month of the year:

- Art
- Music
- Poetry
- Science/ Nature
- Language Arts
- Shakespeare
- Math
- Geography

- Fairy Tale
- Myth
- Tall Tale

---

* Disclaimer: The title for this twelve-month study guide comes from the poem by Henry Wadsworth Longfellow "The Children's Hour". Though it may seem to contradict the fifteen-minute foundation which supports this book, those fifteen-minutes are, in fact, the cornerstone that the Children's Hour is built upon. Simply put: hours are made of minutes.

View your child's life as an hourglass. The sands of time sift and descend like a child sliding into a pit of sand. They are fine moments. Each grain builds upon another grain to form a mountain of sand.

Do you want to build a mountain? Do you want to move mountains? Start with fifteen-minutes. These minutes will slowly and effortlessly build into hours that will build-up your child's character, his memories, and, most of all, his soul.

The fairy tales and folk tales found in each month are not the washed-down Disney versions. These are the best illustrated versions I could find that stay true to the classic fairy tale. Some cautious parents may wish to read them first if they are skeptical of fantasy stories and their undertones or have a sensitive child.

Do not rush through the lists. Books not found or not read before the month is over can be carried over to the next year. This booklist can be spread out into a lifetime study and can be repeated every year with your family's favorites. Each month includes blank lines provided for your family to include any illustrated books found on other historical figures or events not listed in this timeline. Remember, a picture book education is not meant to give a complete education. Its purpose is to spark a fire, fan the flames of one already lit, and enhance a childhood.

The Children's Hour's main purpose is to provide guilt-free reading between parent and child. Its main goal is to lead families to well-developed picture books (for ages 0-100) that coincide with important historical dates, figures, and information.

There will be no revitalization of literature if we do not show the next generation how to *be still* and find the solitude needed for reading and developing their inner self. Do I believe this can be done? Certainly! Let us nurture our children to embrace this as a daily habit for the benefit of our spiritual, mental, and emotional state of mind. Any formation of habit takes roughly six weeks to implement. Setting aside fifteen-minutes each day to read and relax in quiet is something you can do to help your children learn at an early age the virtues of patience and waiting. After six weeks, up the time to thirty minutes. Draw the curtains, dim the lights, and make the reading spots cozy and tranquil. Small children may do puzzles, color, or sculpt with molding clay while Mom or Dad reads aloud; but no one is permitted to disrupt the quiet that reading time begs. Hopefully this time—away from sounds and technology and the world in general—will become a special tradition in your child's childhood memory.

There was no way I could include every worthy book, author, famous person, or folktale in this list. Books are an endless commodity and new ones are being published every day. This list will give you a sense of direction in sharing books and grouping history into the present year with your child. This list will ensure that a day need not go by that you do not share a Children's Hour with your child.

A PICTURE PERFECT EDUCATION
Through the Year

- ❖ *My Grandmother's Clock* by Geraldine McCaughrean/ Stephen Lambert
- ❖ *On This Spot: An Expedition Back Through Time* by Susan E. Goodman/ Lee Christiansen
- ❖ *A Time to Keep* by Tasha Tudor
- ❖ *Around the Year* by Tasha Tudor
- ❖ *The Year at Maple Hill Farm* by Alice and Martin Provensen
- ❖ *Farm Boy's Year* by David McPhail
- ❖ *Around the Year* by Elsa Maartman Beskow
- ❖ *Chicken Soup with Rice: A Book of Months* by Maurice Sendak
- ❖ *Turn! Turn! Turn!* By Wendy Anderson Halperin
- ❖ *Circle of Seasons* by Gerda Muller
- ❖ *A Child's Calendar* by John Updike/ Trina Schart Hyman
- ❖ *Our Colonial Year* by Cheryl Harness
- ❖ *The Stars Will Still Shine* by Cynthia Rylant/ Tiphanie Beeke
- ❖ *Math for All Seasons* by Greg Tang/ Harry Brigg

JANUARY

- *The Little Match Girl* by Hans Christian Andersen/ Rachel Isadora
- (Born January 4, 1809) *A Picture Book of Louis Braille* by David Adler/ John & Alexandra Wallner
- (Commemorated January 8th) *The Battle of New Orleans: The Drummer's Story* by Freddi Williams Evans/ Emile Henriquez
- (Event January 12, 1888) *The Schoolchildren's Blizzard* by Marty Rhodes Figley/ Shelly O. Haas
- *Cleopatra* by Diane Stanley/ Peter Vennema
- (Born January 12, 1908) *Jose! Born to Dance: The Story of Jose Limon* by Susanna Reich/ Raul Colon
- (Born January 15, 1929) *I Have a Dream* by Martin Luther King, Jr./ Foreword by Coretta Scott King
  My Brother Martin: A Sister Remembers by Christine King Farris/ Chris Soentpiet
  Martin's Big Words by Doreen Rappaport/ Bryan Collier
- (Born January 17, 1706) *How Ben Franklin Stole the Lightning* by Rosalyn Schanzer and *Now & Ben: The Modern Inventions of Benjamin Franklin* by Gene Barretta
- (Birth of Anne Bronte ~ January 17, 1820 *The Brontes* by Catherine Brighton

- (Birth of Mack Sennett ~ January 17, 1880) *Mack Made Movies* by Don Brown
- *The Seeds of Peace* by Laura Berkeley/ Alison Dexter
- *Follow the Drinking Gourd* by Jeanette Winter
- *The Rag Coat* by Lauren A. Mills
- (Event January 1856) *Keep the Lights Burning, Abbie* by Peter & Connie Roop/ Peter Hanson
- (Born January 20, 1872) *Julia Morgan Built a Castle* by Celeste Davidson Mannis/ Miles Hyman
- (Born January 27, 1756) *Mozart* by Catherine Brighton
- (Event happened in Winter 1917) *Baby in a Basket* by Gloria Rand/ Ted Rand
- (Born January 28, 1912) *Action Jackson* by Jan Greenberg/ Sandra Jordan/ Robert Andrew Parker
- (Born January 30, 1882) *Make Your Mark, Franklin Roosevelt* by Judith St. George/ Britt Spencer
- (Super Bowl Sunday) *The Greatest Game Ever Played* by Phil Bildner/ Zachary Pullen
- _____
- _____

(Art) *Dreamer from the Village: The Story of Marc Chagall* by Michelle Markel/ Emily Lisker
(Music) *Mozart Finds a Melody* by Stephen Costanza
(Poetry) *Stopping by Woods on a Snowy Evening* by Robert Frost/ Susan Jeffers
(Science/Nature) *A Weed is a Flower: Life of George Washington Carver* by Aliki
(Language Arts) *Eats, Shoots & Leaves* by Lynne Truss/ Bonnie Timmons
(Shakespeare) *Twelfth Night* by Bruce Coville/ Tim Raglin

(Math) *100 School Days* by Anne Rockwell/ Lizzy Rockwell

(Geography) *The Scrambled States of America* by Laurie Keller and *How Much?: Visiting Markets Around the World* by Ted Lewin

(Fairy Tale) *Tattercoats* by Joseph Jacobs/ Margot Tomes and *The Wishing of Biddy Malone* by Joy Cowley/ Christopher Denise and *The Bee-Man of Orn* by Frank R. Stockton/ P.J. Lynch

(Myth) *The Trojan Horse* by Warwick Hutton and *The Trojan Horse* by Albert Lorenz/ Joy Schleh

(Tall Tale) *Pecos Bill* by Steven Kellogg

Notes:

_____

_____

_____

_____

_____

_____

_____

FEBRUARY

- (February 2nd) *Go to Sleep, Groundhog!* by Judy Cox/ Paul Meisel
  Groundhog Day! by Gail Gibbons
- (Born February 3, 1894) *Rockwell: A Boy and his Dog* by Loren Spiotta DiMare/ Cliff Miller
- (Born February 6, 1895) *Home Run: Story of Babe Ruth* by Robert Burleigh/ Mike Wimmer
- (Born February 7, 1812) *Charles Dickens: A Man Who had Great Expectations* by Diane Stanley/ Peter Vennema
- (Born February 7, 1865) *Pioneer Girl ~ Story of Laura Ingalls Wilder* by William Anderson/ Dan Andreasen
- *Tea with Milk* by Allen Say
- (Born February 9, 1985) *Snowflake Bentley* by Jacqueline Briggs Martin
- (Born February 11, 1847) *Thomas Edison* by Lori Mortensen/ Jeffrey Thompson
- (Born February 12, 1809) *Abe Lincoln* by Kay Winters/ Nancy Carpenter
  Abe Lincoln Remembers by Ann Turner/ Wendell Minor

- (Born February 12, 1973) *Barnum Brown: Dinosaur Hunter* by David Sheldon
- (February 14 Feast Day) *Saint Valentine* by Robert Sabuda
- (Born February 14, 1838) *Marvelous Mattie: How Margaret E. Knight Became an Inventor* by Emily Arnold McCully
- (Born February 14, 1891) *Katherine Stinson Otero: High Flyer* by Neila Skinner Petrick/ Daggi Wallace
- (Born February 14, 1847) *A Voice from the Wilderness: The Story of Anna Howard Shaw* by Don Brown
- (Adopted February 15, 1864) *Jim Limber Davis: A Black Orphan in the Confederate White House* by Rickey Pittman/ Judith Hierstein
- (Event February 17, 1864) *The Story of the H.L. Hunley and Queenie's Coin* by Fran Hawk/ Dan Nance
- (Born February 19, 1473) *Nicolaus Copernicus: The Earth is a Planet* by Dennis B. Fradin/ Cynthia Von Buhler
- (President's Day) *So You Want to Be President?* by Judith St. George/ David Small
  Let's Celebrate President's Day by Connie and Peter Roop
- (Born February 22, 1732) *George Washington* by James Giblin/ Michael Dooling
  George Washington's Teeth by Deborah Chandra/ Madeleine Comora
- *Musicians of the Sun* by Gerald McDermott
- *A New Coat for Anna* by Harriet Ziefert/ Anita Lobel
- *Rain Makes Applesauce* by Julian Schneer/ Marvin Bileck
- *Katie's Trunk* by Ann Turner/ Ronald Himler
- (Birth of Buffalo Bill Cody ~ February 26, 1845) *The*

Sweetwater Run by Andrew Glass
- (Born February 27, 1897) *When Marian Sang* by Pam Munoz Ryan/ Brian Selznick
- (Birth of J.W. Williams ~ February 28, 1929) *Mr. Williams* by Karen Barbour

- _____
- _____
- _____

(Art) *Math-terpieces* by Greg Tang/ Greg Paprocki and *Grandfather Tang's Story* by Ann Tompert/ Robert Andrew Parker

(Music) *Zin! Zin! Zin! A Violin* by Lloyd Moss/ Marjorie Priceman

(Poetry) *Birches* by Robert Frost/ Ed Young

(Language Arts) *Monkey Business* by Wallace Edwards and *First Things First* by Betty Fraser

(Science/Nature) *The Listening Walk* by Paul Showers/ Aliki

(Shakespeare) *The Winter's Tale* by Bruce Coville/ LeUyen Pham

(Math) *Grandpa Gazillion's Number Yard* by Laurie Keller and *The Best of Times* by Greg Tang/ Harry Briggs

(Geography) *The Travels of Benjamin of Tudela: Through Three Continents in the Twelfth Century* by Uri Shulevitz

(Fairy Tale) *Mother Holly* by Brothers Grimm/ John Warren Stewig/ Johanna Westerman

(Myth) *Cupid and Psyche* by M. Charlotte Craft/ K.Y. Craft and *The Arrow and the Lamp: The Story of Psyche* by Margaret Hodges/ Donna Diamond

(Tall Tale) *Swamp Angel* by Anne Isaacs/ Paul O. Zelinsky

Notes:

_____

_____

_____

_____

_____

MARCH

- *A Packet of Seeds* by Deborah Hopkinson/ Bethanne Andersen
- *The Heart of the Wood* by Marguerite W. Davol/ Sheila Hamanaka
- *Cold Feet* by Cynthia DeFelice/ Robert Andrew Parker
- (Born March 2, 1859) *Sholom's Treasure: How Sholom Aleichem Became a Writer* by Erica Silverman/ Mordicai Gerstein

- (Born March 2, 1904) *The Boy on Fairfield Street* by Kathleen Krull/ Steve Johnson & Lou Fancher
- (Born March 3, 1847) *Alexander Graham Bell* by Victoria Sherrow/ Elaine Verstraete
- (Born March 4, 1747) *Hero on Horseback: The Story of Casimir Pulaski* by David R. Collins/ Larry Nolte
- (Kite Flying Event 1847) *The Flight of the Union* by Tekla White/ Ralph Ramstad
- *Jamie O'Rourke and the Pooka* by Tomie dePaola
- *Spring Story* by Jill Barklem
- (Born March 6, 1475) *Michelangelo* by Diane Stanley
- (Battle of the Alamo ~ March 6, 1836) *Susanna of the Alamo* by John Jakes/ Paul Bacon
- (Born March 14, 1879) *Odd Boy Out: Young Albert Einstein* by Don Brown
- (March 17 Feast Day) *Patrick Patron Saint of Ireland* by Tomie dePaola
- (Married March 17, 1905) *Franklin & Eleanor* by Cheryl Harness
- (March 19 Feast Day) *Song of the Swallows* by Leo Politi
- (Born March 19, 1864) *Cowboy Charlie: The Story of Charles M. Russell* by Jeanette Winter
- *Montezuma & the Fall of the Aztecs* by Eric A. Kimmel/ Daniel San Souci
- (Born March 21, 1685) *Bach's Big Adventure* by Sallie Ketcham/ Timothy Bush
- *The Springs of Joy* by Tasha Tudor
- (Birth of Fannie Farmer ~ March 23, 1857) *Fannie in the Kitchen* by Deborah Hopkinson/ Nancy Carpenter
- *Viking Longship* by Mick Manning/ Birta Granstrom
- (Born March 24, 1834) *The Last River: John Wesley Powell and the Colorado River Exploring Expedition* by Stuart Waldman
- (Born March 24, 1874) *The Secret of the Great*

69

Houdini by Robert Burleigh/ Leonid Gore
- *On Passover* by Cathy Goldberg Fishman/ Melanie W. Hall
- *Cloudy with a Chance of Meatballs* by Judi Barrett/ Ron Barrett
- *Let's Go!: The Story of Getting from There to Here* by Lizann Flatt/ Scott Ritchie
- (Born March 31, 1927) *Harvesting Hope: the Story of Cesar Chavez* by Kathleen Krull/ Yuyi Morales
- _____
- _____
- _____

(Art) *The Genius of Leonardo* by Guido Visconti/ Bimba Landmann
(Music) *Meet the Orchestra* by Ann Hayes/ Karmen Thompson
(Poetry) *R is for Rhyme* by Judy Young/ Victor Juhasz and *Wynken, Blynken, and Nod* by Eugene Field illustrated versions by Giselle Potter/ David Mcphail/ Johanna Westerman
(Language Arts) *Max's Words* by Kate Banks/ Boris Kulikov
(Science/Nature) *Anna's Table* by Eve Bunting/ Taia Morley
(Shakespeare) *Romero and Juliet* by Bruce Coville/ Dennis Nolan
(Math) *Archimedes: Ancient Greek Mathematician* by Susan Katz Keating/ Stefano Tartarotti
(Geography) *Somewhere in the World Right Now* by Stacey Schuett
(Fairy Tale) *Little Red Riding Hood* by the Brothers Grimm/ Trina Schart Hyman and *Snow White and Rose Red* by the Brothers Grimm/ Barbara Cooney
(Myth) *The Trouble with Wishes* by Diane Stanley
(Tall Tale) *Paul Bunyan* by Steven Kellogg

Notes:

_____

_____

_____

_____

_____

_____

_____

_____

APRIL

- (Born April 2, 1805) *The Perfect Wizard: Hans Christian Andersen* by Jane Yolen/ Dennis Nolan

- (Pony Express Event ~ April 3, 1860) *Ride Like the Wind: A Tale of the Pony Express* by Bernie Fuchs
  They're Off!: Story of the Pony Express by Cheryl Harness
  Bronco Charlies and the Pony Express by Marlene Targ Brill/ Craig Orback
- (Event April 1942) *Ballet of the Elephants* by Leda Schubert/ Robert Andrew Parker
- (Birth of Booker T. Washington ~ April 5, 1856) *More than Anything Else* by Marie Bradby/ Chris Soentpiet
- (Born April 5, 1934) *Hank Aaron: Brave in Every Way* by Peter Golenbock/ Paul Lee
- (Invasion of Iraq April 6, 2003) *Librarian of Basra* by Jeanette Winter
- (Surrender at Appomatox April 9, 1865) *The Silent Witness* by Robin Friedman/ Claire A. Nivola
- (Easter) *Little Rose of Sharon* by Nan Gurley/ Tim Jonke
  The Tale of Three Trees by Angela Elwell Hunt
  A Tale for Easter by Tasha Tudor
  Petook: An Easter Story by Houselander/ dePaola
- *The Velveteen Rabbit* by Margery Williams/ William Nicholson (another one with pictures by Elizabeth Miles) (another one illustrated by Michael Hague)
- *The Country Bunny and the Little Gold Shoes* by DuBose Heyward/ Marjorie Hack
- (Born April 13, 1743) *Thomas Jefferson* by James Giblin/ Michael Dooling
  When Mr. Jefferson Came to Philadelphia by Ann Turner/ Mark Hess
- (Event April 14, 1912) *Pig on the Titanic: A True Story* by Gary Crew/ Bruce Whatley
- (Born April 15, 1452) *Leonardo Da Vinci* by Diane Stanley

72

- (Born April 15, 1894) *Bessie Smith and the Night Riders* by Sue Stauffacher/ John Holyfield
- (Birth of Isaac Burns Murphy ~ April 16, 1861) *Perfect Timing* by Patsi B. Trollinger/ Jerome Lagarrigne
- (Event April 18-19, 1775) *Paul Revere's Midnight Ride* by Stephen Krensky/ Greg Harlin
- (Event April 18, 1865) *Willie McLean and the Civil War Surrender* by Candice Ransom/ Jeni Reeves
- (Event April 18, 1906) *Earthquake* by Molly Lee/ Yangsook Choi
- (Born April 20, 1739) *The Flower Hunter: William Bartram, America's First Naturalist* by Deborah Kogan Ray
- (Birth of Charlotte Bronte ~ Born April 21, 1816) *Glass Town* by Michael Bedard/ Laura Fernandez/ Rick Jacobson
- (Born April 21, 1838/ Earth Day) *Squirrel and John Muir* by Emily Arnold McCully
  John Muir: America's First Environmentalist by Kathryn Lasky/ Stan Fellows
- (April 23rd) *St. George and the Dragon* by Margaret Hodges/ Trina Schart Hyman
- (Born April 23, 1564) *The Bard of Avon* by Diane Stanley
- *The Kitchen Knight* by Margaret Hodges/ Trina Schart Hyman
- (Born April 26, 1785) *The Boy Who Drew Birds: A Story of John James Audubon* by Jacqueline Davies/ Melissa Sweet
- (Event April 26, 1777) *Sybil Ludington's Midnight Ride* by Marsha Amstel/Ellen Beier
- (Event April 26, 1869) *Ten Mile Day: The Building of the Transcontinental Railroad* by Mary Ann Fraser

- (April 27, 1937/ Completion of Golden Gate Bridge) *Pop's Bridge* by Eve Bunting/ C.F. Payne
- (Event April 1933) *Amelia & Eleanor Go for a Ride* by Pam Munoz Ryan/ Brian Selznick
- _____
- _____
- _____

(Art) *The Art Lesson* by Tomie dePaola
(Music) *The Story of the Incredible Orchestra* by Bruce Koscielniak
(Poetry) *The Midnight Ride of Paul Revere* by Henry Wadsworth Longfellow/ Christopher Bing (also book illustrated by Ted Rand)
(Language Arts) *Mom and Dad are Palindromes* by Mark Shulman/ Adam McCauley
(Science/Nature) *A Drop around the World* by Barbara Shaw McKinney/ Michael Maydak
(Shakespeare) *All the World's a Stage* by Rebecca Piatt Davidson/ Anita Lobel
(Math) *The Grapes of Math* and *Math Appeal* and *Math Potatoes* by Greg Tang/ Harry Briggs
(Geography) *The World Made New* by Marc Aronson/ John W. Gleen
(Fairy Tale) *The Golden Goose* by Brothers Grimm/ Uri Shulevitz and *The Magic Crystal* by Brigitte Weninger/ Robert Ingpen
(Myth) *Pandora* by Robert Burleigh/ Raul Colon and *Pandora's Box: A Greek Myth* by Jean Marzollo
(Tall Tale) *Mike Fink* by Steven Kellogg

MAY

- (May 1, 1931/ Empire State Building Opened) *Sky Boys* by Deborah Hopkinson/ James Ransome
- *Oh, the Places You'll Go!* by Dr. Seuss
- (True Event/ 1914) *Mailing May* by Michael O. Tunnell/ Ted Rand
- *Miss Rumphius* by Barbara Cooney
- (804 A.D.) *The Sailor Who Captured the Sea: A Story of the Book of Kells* by Deborah Nourse Lattimore
- (Event May 5, 1862) *Viva Mexico! The Story of Benito Juarez and Cinco de Mayo* by Argentina Palacios/ Alex Haley/ Howard Berelson

75

- (Born May 5, 1864) *Nellie Bly's Monkey* by Joan W. Blos/ Catherine Stock
- (Event May 6, 1937) *The Hindenburg* by Patrick O'Brien
- (Born May 11, 1875) *Brave Harriet: The First Woman to Fly the English Channel* by Marissa Moss/ C.F. Payne
- (Born May 17, 1866) *Strange Mr. Satie* by M.T. Anderson/ Petra Mathers
- (Born May 18, 1920) *Karol from Poland* by M. Leonora Wilson/ Carla Koch
- (Born May 21, 1799) *Rare Treasure: Mary Anning and her Remarkable Discoveries* by Don Brown and *Stone Girl, Bone Girl* by Laurence Anholt/ Sheila Moxley
- (Born May 22, 1844) *Mary Cassatt: Impressionist Painter* by Lois V. Harris
- (Opening Ceremony ~ May 24, 1883) *Brooklyn Bridge* by Lynn Curlee
- *Twenty-One Elephants and Still Standing* by April Jones Prince/ Francois Roca
- *Twenty-One Elephants* by Phil Bildner/ LeUyen Pham
- (Born May 25, 1803) *Mr. Emerson's Cook* by Judith Bryon Schachner
- (Born May 26, 1877) *Isadora Dances* by Rachel Isadora
- (Born May 27, 1907) *Rachel: The Story of Rachel Carson* by Amy Ehrlich/ Wendell Minor and *Rachel Carson* by Thomas Locker/ Joseph Bruchac
- *A Place Where Sunflowers Grow* by Amy Lee-Tai/ Felicia Hoshino
- (1847) *Apples to Oregon* by Deborah Hopkinson/ Nancy Carpenter
- (Memorial Day) *The Wall* by Eve Bunting/ Ronald Himler

America's White Table by Margot Theis Raven/ Mike Benny
- *Dr. White* by Jane Goodall/ Julie Litty
- *Miss Opal's Auction* by Susan Vizurraga/ Mark Graham
- (May 30th Feast Day) *Joan of Arc: The Lily Maid* by Margaret Hodges/ Robert Rayevsky *Joan of Arc* by Diane Stanley

- _____
- _____
- _____

(**Art**) *Fancy That* by Esther Hershenhorn/ Megan Lloyd and *The Day the Picture Man Came* by Faye Gibbons/ Sherry Meidell

(**Music**) *Ah, Music!* by Aliki

(**Poetry**) (Memorial Day) *In Flander's Field: The Story of the Poem by John McCrae* by Linda Granfield/ Janet Wilson

(**Language Arts**) *The Boy Who Loved Words* by Roni Schotter/ Giselle Potter

(**Science/Nature**) *The Story of Salt* by Mark Kurlansky/ S.D. Schindler and *It's Disgusting and We Ate it!* by James Solheim/ Eric Brace

(**Shakespeare**) *Hear, Hear, Mr. Shakespeare* by Bruce Koscielniak

(**Math**) *How the Second Grade Got $8,205.50 to Visit the Statue of Liberty* by Nathan Zimelman/Bill Slavin

(**Geography**) *Madlenka* by Peter Sis

(**Fairy Tale**) *The White Cat* by Robert D. San Souci/ Gennady Spirin and *The Well at the End of the World* by Robert D. San Souci/ Rebecca Walsh

(**Myth**) *Atlantis: The Legend of the Lost City* by Christina Balit

(**Tall Tale**) *Sally Ann Thunder Whirlwind Crockett* by Steven Kellogg

77

JUNE

- *The Sandcastle* by M. P. Robertson
- *Sea Story* by Jill Barklem
- *The Sea Chest* by Toni Buzzeo/ Mary GrandPre
- (June 9, 1909/ Began Journey Across America) *Alice Ramsey's Grand Adventure* by Don Brown
- (1896-1910) *Sailing Home: A Story of a Childhood at Sea* by Gloria and Ted Rand
- *The Mutiny on the Bounty* by Patrick O'Brien
- (World War II---Holocaust) *The Cats in Krasinski Square* by Karen Hesse/ Wendy Watson
- (Born June 12, 1929) *Anne Frank* by Josephine Poole/ Angela Barrett and *Anne Frank* by Yona Zeldis McDonough/ Malcah Zeldis

78

- *Across the Alley* by Richard Michelson/ E.B. Lewis
- *My Little Artist* by Donna Green
- (Summer 1899) *Kid Blink Beats the World* by Don Brown
- (Flag Day ~ June 14th) *Keep on Sewing, Betsy Ross* by Michael Dahl/ Sandra D'Antonio
- (Father's Day) *A Father's Song* by Janet Lawler/ Lucy Corvino
- *Leah's Pony* by Elizabeth Friedrich/ Michael Garland
- (*Event June 26, 1284) *Robert Browning's the Pied Piper of Hamelin* illustrated by Bud Peen and another one illustrated by Kate Greenaway
- (Born June 27, 1880) *A Picture Book of Helen Keller* by David Adler/ John & Alexandra Wallner
- *The Last Princess (Story of Princess Ka'iulani of Hawai'i)* by Fay Stanley/ Diane Stanley
- *The Bee Tree* by Patricia Polacco
- *Secret of the Sphinx* by James Giblin/ Bagram Ibatoulline
- *Dr. Welch and the Great Grape Story* by Mary Lou Carney/ Sherry Meidell
- *Sequoyah* by James Rumford
- *The Shaman's Apprentice: A Tale of the Amazon Rain Forest* by Lynne Cherry/ Mark J. Plotkin
- *Appalachia: The Voices of Sleeping Birds* and *When I Was Young in the Mountains* by Cynthia Rylant
- *Rikki-Tikki-Tavi* by Rudyard Kipling/ Jerry Pinkney
- *Tikki Tikki Tembo* by Arlene Mosel/ Blair Lent
- *The Librarian Who Measured the Earth* by Kathryn Lasky

(* Various dates of the actual event are recorded; the dated listed in "The Children's Hour" is taken from Wikipedia.)

- _____
- _____
- _____

(Art) *Opt: An Illusionary Tale* by Arline & Joseph Baum and *Spread Your Wings and Fly: An Origami Fold-and-Tell Story* by Mary Chloe Schoolcraft Saunders/ Carla McGregor Mihelich

(Music) *Two Scarlet Songbirds: A Story of Anton Dvorak* by Carole Lexa Schaefer/ Elizabeth Rosen

(Poetry) *Casey at the Bat* by Ernest Lawrence Thayer/ Illustrated by Christopher Bing/ C.F. Payne/ Steve Johnson & Lou Fancher/ Patricia Polacco

(Language Arts) Through the summer read any of Brian P. Cleary's clever language arts books or Ruth Heller's beautiful carousel-of-colors language arts books.

(Science/Nature) *Beachcombing: Exploring the Seashore* by Jim Arnosky

(Shakespeare) *A Midnight Summer's Dream* by Bruce Coville/ Dennis Nolan

(Math) *Lemonade for Sale* by Stuart J. Murphey/ Tricia Tusa and *What's Your Angle, Pythagoras?* by Julie Ellis/ Phyllis Hornung

(Geography) *Taj Mahal* by Caroline Arnold/ Madeleine Comora/ Rahal Bhaghan

(Fairy Tale) *The Pied Piper of Hamelin* by Michele Lemieux and another one by Mercer Mayer

(Myth) *The Hero and the Minotaur* by Robert Byrd

(Tall Tale) *John Henry* by Julius Lester/ Jerry Pinkney

JULY

- (Independence Day) *Red, White, and Blue* by John Herman/ Robin Roraback
  We the Kids by David Catrow
  A Fourth of July on the Plains by Jean Van Leeuwen/ Henri Sorensen
  The Fourth of July Story by Alice Dalgliesh/ Marie Nonnast
- *Purple Mountains Majesties* by Barbara Younger/ Stacey Schuett

- *America the Beautiful* by Katharine Lee Bates/ Wendell Minor
- *How to Bake an American Pie* by Karma Wilson/ Raul Colon
- *By Dawn's Early Light* by Steven Kroll/ Dan Andreasen
- *Saving the Liberty Bell* by Megan McDonald/ Marsha Gray Carrington
  Saving the Liberty Bell by Marty Rhodes Figley/ Kevin Lepp
- *The Girl on the High-Diving Horse* by Linda Oatman High/ Ted Lewin
- (Battle took place on July 4, 1863) *We Played Marbles* by Tres Seymour/ Dan Andreasen
- (Groundbreaking of Erie Canel, July 4, 1817) *Amazing Impossible Erie Canal* by Cheryl Harness
- (Event July 6, 1881) *Kate Shelley: Bound for Legend* by Robert D. San Souci/ Max Ginsburg and *Kate Shelley and the Midnight Express* by Margaret K. Wetterer/ Karen Ritz
- (Born July 10, 1759) *Redoute' ~ The Man Who Painted Flowers* by Carolyn Croll
- (Born July 12, 1817) *Henry David's House* by Steven Schnur/ Peter Fiore
  The Trouble with Henry: A Tale of Walden Pond by Deborah O'Neal/ Angela Westengard/ S.D. Schindler
  (Born July 12, 1984) *A Weed is a Flower: The Life of George Washington Carver* by Aliki
- (Born July 16, 1888) *Shoeless Joe and Black Betsy* by Phil Bildner/ C.F. Payne
- (Summer 1951) *The Shot Heard Round the World* by Phil Bildner/ C.F. Payne
- (Born July 18, 1867) *The Heroine of the Titanic* by Joan W. Blos/ Tennessee Dixon

- (Born July 20, 1822) *Gregor Mendel: The Friar Who Grew Peas* by Cheryl Bardoe/ Jos. A. Smith
- (Born July 23, 1798) *Jane Wilkinson Long: Texas Pioneer* by Neila Skinner Petrick/ Joyce Haynes
- (July 25th Feast Day) *Christopher, the Holy Giant* by Tomie dePaola
- (Event July 25, 1909) *The Glorious Flight: Across the English Channel with Louis Bleriot* by Alice Provensen/ Martin Provensen
- (Founded July 1911) *Lost City: The Discovery of Machu Picchu* by Ted Lewin
- (Born July 27, 1975) *Out of the Ballpark* by Alex Rodriquez/ Frank Morrison
- (Event July 28, 1755) *Evangeline for Children* by Alice Couvillon/ Elizabeth Moore/ Alison Davis Lyne *Jean-Paul Hebert Was There* by Sheila Hebert-Collins/ John W. Bergeron
- (Born on July 28, 1866) *Beatrix Potter* by Alexandra Wallner
  The True Story of Peter Rabbit by Jane Johnson
- *You Forgot Your Skirt, Amelia Bloomer!* by Shana Corey/ Chesley McLaren
- _____
- _____
- _____

(Art) *The Gentleman and the Kitchen Maid* by Diane Stanley/ Dennis Nolan
(Music) *Purple Mountain Majesties* by Barbara Younger/ Stacey Schuett
(Poetry) *The Brook* by Alfred Tennyson/ Charles Micucci
(Language Arts) Through the summer read any of Brian P. Cleary's clever language arts books or Ruth Heller's beautiful carousel-of-colors language arts books.

(Science/Nature) *The Same Sun was in the Sky* by Denise Webb/ Walter Porter

(Shakespeare) *William Shakespeare & the Globe* by Aliki and *Shakespeare* by Peter Chrisp

(Math) *Patterns in Peru: An Adventure in Patterning* by Cindy Neuschwander/ Bryan Langdo

(Geography) *Mapping Penny's World* by Loreen Leedy

(Fairy Tale) *The Wild Swans* by Hans Christian Andersen/ Naomi Lewis/ Anne Yvonne Gilbert and *Thumbelina* by Hans Christian Andersen/ Lauren Mills

(Myth) *Young Arthur* by Robert D. San Souci/ Jamichael Henterly

(Tall Tale) *Dona Flor: A Tall Tale about a Giant Woman with a Great Big Heart* by Pat Mora/ Raul Colon

Notes:

_____

_____

_____

_____

_____

_____

_____

_____

AUGUST

- (Hot August Day in 79 A.D.) *Escape from Pompeii* by Christina Balit
- (Born August 1, 1818) *Maria's Comet* by Deborah Hopkinson/ Deborah Lanino
- (Born August 1, 1920) *Sixteen Years in Sixteen Seconds: The Sammy Lee Story* by Paula Yoo/ Dom Lee
- *A Spoon for Every Bite* by Joe Hayes/ Rebecca Leer
- *The Cataract of Lodore* by Robert Southey/ Mordicai Gerstein
- *Train to Somewheres* by Eve Bunting/ Ronald Himler
- (Olympic Event August 5, 1936) *Jesse Owens: Fastest Man Alive* by Carole Boston Weatherford/ Eric Velasquen
- *Black Sky River* by Tres Seymour/ Dan Andreasen
- (Born August 8, 1814) *I Could Do That!: Esther Morris Gets Women the Vote* by Linda Arms White/ Nancy Carpenter and *When Esther Morris Headed West* by Connie Nordhielm Wooldridge/ Jacqueline Rogers
- (Birth of Florence Martus ~ August 8, 1868) *The Waving Girl* by J. B. Nicholas/ Joan C. Waites
- (Born August 13, 1860) *Shooting for the Moon: the Amazing Life and Times of Annie Oakley* Stephen Krensky/ Bernie Fuchs
- (Born August 17, 1971) *Play Ball!* by Jorge Posada/ Robert Burleigh/ Raul Colon

- (Born August 18, 1934) *Roberto Clemente: Pride of the Pittsburgh Pirates* by Jonah Winter/ Raul Colon
- (Event August 19, 1991) *Hurricane!* by Corinne Demas/ Lenice Strohmeier
- (Born August 19, 1871 & April 16, 1867) *The Wondrous Whirligig: The Wright Brothers First Flying Machine* by Andrew Glass
- (Born August 19, 1874) *My Brothers' Flying Machine: Wilbur, Orville, and Me* by Jane Yolen/ Jim Burke
- *The Way West* by Amelia Stewart Knight/ Michael McCurdy
- (Burning of White House August 24, 1814) *Dolley Madison Saves George Washington* by Don Brown
- (Event August 24, 1853) *George Crum and the Saratoga Chip* by Gaylia Taylor/ Frank Morrison
- (Born August 27, 1910) *Stories Told by Mother Teresa* by Teresa/ Edward LeJoly/ Jaya Chaliha/ Allan Drummond
  Mother Teresa by Demi
- (Born August 30, 1893) *Huey P. Long: Talker and Doer* by David R. Collins/ Jack Smith
- *What Charlie Heard* by Mordicai Gerstein
- *All the Secrets in the World* by Jane Yolen/ Leslie Baker
- *The Bat Boy & His Violin* by Gavin Curtis/ E. B. Lewis
- *Something from Nothing* by Phoebe Gilman
- *Why Mosquitoes Buzz in People's Ears* by Verna Aardema/ Leo & Diane Dillon
- *Five Secrets in a Box* by Catherine Brighton
- *One Grain of Rice* by Demi
- _____
- _____
- _____

(Art) *The Boy Who Loved to Draw: Benjamin West* by Barbara Brenner/ Olivier Dunrea

(Music) *The Philharmonic Gets Dressed* by Karla Kuskin/ Marc Simont

(Poetry) *The Cow in Apple Time* by Robert Frost/ Dean Yeagle and *The Runaway* by Robert Frost/ Glenna Lang

(Language Arts) Through the summer read any of Brian P. Cleary's clever language arts books or Ruth Heller's beautiful carousel-of-colors language arts books.

(Science/Nature) *Of Numbers and Stars: The Story of Hypatia* by D. Anne Love/ Pam Paparone

(Shakespeare) *MacBeth* by Bruce Coville/ Gary Kelley

(Math) *Sir Cumference and the Great Knight of Angleland* by Cindy Neuschwander/ Wayne Geehan and *Sir Cumference and the Isle of Immeter* by Cindy Neuschwander/ Wayne Geehan

(Geography) *P is for Passport: A World Alphabet* by Devin Scillian/

(Fairy Tale) *Hansel and Gretel* by Rika Lesser/ Paul O. Zelinsky

(Myth) *Stolen Thunder: A Norse Myth* by Shirley Climo/ Alexander Koshkin

(Tall Tale) *The Hired Hand* by Robert D. San Souci/ Jerry Pinkney

---

Notes:

_____

_____

_____

SEPTEMBER

- *It's Fall* by Linda Glaser
- (Grandparent's Day---First Sunday after Labor Day) *Grandpa for Sale* by Dotti Enderle/ Vicki Sansum/ T. Kyle Gentry
- *Grandfather's Wrinkles* by Kathryn England/ Richard McFarland
- (Born September 4, 1908) *Richard Wright and the Library Card* by William Miller/ Gregory Christie
- (Birth Unknown/ Died September 5, 1877) *Crazy Horse's Vision* by Joseph Bruchac/ S.D. Nelson
- *Apple Picking Time* by Michele B. Slawson/ Deborah Kogan Ray
- *An Apple for Harriet Tubman* by Glennette Tilley Turner/ Susan Keeter
- (Born 1773) *The Escape of Oney Judge: Martha Washington's Slave Finds Freedom* by Emily Arnold McCully
- (Born September 7, 1533) *Good Queen Bess: The Story of Elizabeth I of England* by Diane Stanley/ Peter Vennema
- (Born September 7, 1936) *Buddy: The Story of Buddy Holly* by Anne Bustard/ Kyle Cyrus

- *The Bravest of Us All* by Marsha Diane Arnold/ Brad Sneed
- (Remembrance of September 11, 2001) *The Man Who Walked Between The Towers* by Mordicai Gerstein
- (September 11, 2001) *The Little Chapel that Stood* by A.B. Curtiss/ Mirto Golino
  Fireboat: The Heroic Adventures of John J. Harvey by Maira Kalman
- *Jingle Dancer* by Cynthia Leitich Smith/ Cornelius Van Wright/ Ying-Hwa Hu
- *A Song for Lena* by Hilary Horder Hippely/ Leslie Baker
- (Born September 15, 1857) *The President and Mom's Apple Pie* by Michael Garland
- (Event September 19, 1783) *Hot Air: The Mostly True Story of the First Hot-Air Balloon Ride* by Marjorie Priceman
- (Born September 25, 1847) *Vinnie and Abraham* by Dawn Fitzgerald/ Catherine Stock
- (Born September 26th) *Johnny Appleseed books* by Will Moses/ Aliki/ Steven Kellogg/ Reeve Linbergh & Kathy Jakobsen/ Stephen & Rosemary Benet & Steven Schindler
- *The Story of Ferdinand* by Munro Leaf
- *A Band of Angels, a Story Inspired by the Jubilee Singers* by Deborah Hopkinson/ Raul Colon
- *Mandy* by Barbara D. Booth/ Jim LaMarche
- *Over in the Meadow* by Ezra Jack Keats
- *The Milkman's Boy* by Donald Hall/ Greg Shed
- *Autumn Story* by Jill Barklem
- *Sam and the Tigers* by Julius Lester/ Jerry Pinkney
- *Little Country Town* by Jandelyn Southwell/ Kay Chorao
- *The Apple Pie that Papa Baked* by Lauren Thompson/ Jonathan Bean

- _____
- _____
- _____

(Art) *The Magical Garden of Claude Monet* by Laurence Anholt

(Music) *The Cello of Mr. O* by Jane Cutler/ Greg Couch

(Poetry) *Qu'Appelle* by David Bouchard/ Michael Lonechild and *Caedmon's Song* by Ruth Ashby/ Bill Slavin

(Language Arts) *Dear Deer: A Book of Homophones* by Gene Barretta

(Science/Nature) *Into the Woods* by Robert Burleigh/ Wendell Minor

(Shakespeare) *The Tempest* by Bruce Coville/ Ruth Sanderson

(Math) *Sir Cumference and the Sword in the Cone* by Cindy Neuschwander/ Wayne Geehan and *Sir Cumference and the First Round Table* by Cindy Neuschwander/ Wayne Geehan

(Geography) *How to Make an Apple Pie & See the World* by Marjorie Priceman

(Fairy Tale) *The Tale of the Firebird* by Gennady Spirin and *The Firebird: A Traditional Russian Folktale* by C.J. Moore/ Jindra Capek

(Myth) *Atalanta's Race: a Greek Myth* by Shirley Climo/ Alexander Koshkin

(Tall Tale) *Johnny Appleseed* by Steven Kellogg

Notes:
_____
_____

OCTOBER

- (Event October 4, 1759) *Malian's Song* by Marge Bruchac/ William Maughan
- (Arrival October 1815) *My Napoleon* by Catherine Brighton
- (Born October 11, 1884) *Eleanor* by Barbara Cooney
- (Event October 11, 1896) *Rescue on the Outer Banks* by Candice F. Ransom/ Karen Ritz
- *Emma* by Wendy Kesselman/ Barbara Cooney
- (Columbus Observance October 12th) *Encounter* by Jane Yolen/ David Shannon
  In 1492 by Jean Marzollo
- (Born October 13, 1754) *They Called Her Molly Pitcher* by Anne Rockwell/ Cynthia von Buhler
- (Born October 13, 1862) *Uncommon Traveler: Mary Kingsley in Africa* by Don Brown
- (Born October 14, 1644) *William Penn: Founder of Pennsylvania* by Steven Kroll/ Ronald Himler
- (Born October 20, 1874) *What Charlie Heard* by Mordicai Gerstein
- (Born October 21, 1917) *Dizzy* by Jonah Winter/ Sean Qualls
- (Born October 22, 1734) *Daniel Boone: Trailblazer* by Nancy Kelly Allen/ Joan C. Waites

- (Born October 24, 1871) *Louis Sockalexis: Native American Baseball Pioneer* by Bill Wise/ Bill Farnsworth
- (Born October 27, 1858) *You're on Your Way, Teddy Roosevelt* by Judith St. George/ Matt Faulkner
- *Nutmeg* by David Lucas
- (Official Dedication October 28, 1886) *The Story of the Statue of Liberty* by Betsy and Guilio Maestro
- (Event October 29, 1787) *Mozart Tonight* by Julie Downing
- (Event October 30, 1938) *Aliens are Coming! The True Account of the 1938 War of the Worlds Radio Broadcast* by Meghan McCarthy
- (October 31) *Pumpkin Moonshine* by Tasha Tudor
- *Rip Van Winkle* by Washington Irving/ John Howe (another book by Will Moses)
- *Georgie* by Robert Bright
- *Ghosts of the Civil War* by Cheryl Harness
- *Ghosts of the White House* by Cheryl Harness
- *Ghosts of the Twentieth Century* by Cheryl Harness
- *Johann Gutenberg and the Amazing Printing Press* by Bruce Koscielniak
- *Where Do Balloons Go?* by Jamie Lee Curtis/ Laura Cornell
- *The Legend of Sleepy Hollow* by Washington Irving/ Will Moses
- *The Ghost of Nicholas Greebe* by Tony Johnston/ S. D. Schindler
- *Wicked Jack* by Connie Nordhielm Wooldridge/ Will Hillenbrand
- *Ghost Ship* by Mary Higgins Clark/ Wendell Minor
- *The Great Pumpkin Switch* by Megan McDonald/ Ted Lewin

- _____
- _____
- _____

(Art) *A Boy Named Giotto* by Paolo Guarnieri/ Bimba Landmann and *Mario's Angels: A Story About the Artist Giotto* by Mary Arrigan/ Gillian McClure and *Michelangelo's Surprise* by Tony Parillo
(Music) *M is for Music* by Kathleen Krull/ Stacy Innerst and *M is for Melody* by Kathy-Jo Wargin/ Katherine Larson
(Poetry) *When the Frost is on the Punkin* by James Whitcomb Riley/ Glenna Lang
(Language Arts) *Mine, All Mine: A Book about Pronouns* by Ruth Heller
(Science/Nature) *Crinkleroot's Guide to Walking in Wild Places* by Jim Arnosky
(Shakespeare) *Hamlet* by Bruce Coville/ Leonid Gore
(Math) *Mummy Math: An Adventure in Geometry* by Cindy Neuschwander/ Bryan Langdo and *Math Curse* by Jon Scieszka/ Lane Smith
(Geography) *Talking Walls* by Margy Burns Knight/ Anne Sibley O'Brien
(Fairy Tale) *The Red Heels* by Robert D. San Souci/ Gary Kelley
(Myth) *The Night the Moon Fell: A Maya Myth* by Pat Mora/ Domi and *Moon's Cloud Blanket* by Rose Anne St. Romain/ Joan C. Waites
(Tall Tale) *Bewildered for Three Days: As to Why Daniel Boone Never Wore His Coonskin Cap* by Andrew Glass

NOVEMBER

- (November 1 and 2/ Day of the Dead) *Spirit of Tio Fernando* by Janice Levy/ Morella Fuenmayor
- *Carnival of the Animals* by Saint-Saens by Barry Carson Turner/ Sue Williams
- (Born November 9, 1731) *Dear Benjamin Banneker* by Andrea Davis Pinkney/ Brian Pinkney
- (November 11th---Veteran's Day) *America's White Table* by Margot Theis Raven/ Mike Benny

- *Think Pink* by Olga Cossi/ Lea Anne Clarke
- *Molly Bannaky* by Alice McGill/ Chris K. Soentpiet
- *Thank You, Sarah: The Woman Who Saved Thanksgiving* by Laurie Halse Anderson/ Matt Faulkner
- (Event November 10, 1975) *The Edmund Fitzgerald: Song of the Bell* by Kathy-Jo Wargin/ Gijsbert Van Frankenhuyzen
- (Born November 12, 1840) *Little Sap and Monsieur Rodin* by Michelle Lord/ Felicia Hoshino
- *Cranberry Thanksgiving* by Wende/ Harry Devlin
- *Baseball Saved Us* by Ken Mochizuki/ Dom Lee
- (Event Happened November 14, 1960) *The Story of Ruby Bridges* by Robert Coles/ George Ford
- (Born November 15, 1887) *Georgia's Bones* by Jen Bryant/ Bethanne Anderson
- (November 19, 1863)*The Gettysburg Address* by Abraham Lincoln/ illustrated by Michael McCurdy
- (Event November 19, 1916) *Ruth Law Thrills a Nation* by Don Brown
- (Thanksgiving) *Squanto's Journey: The Story of the First Thanksgiving* by Joseph Bruchac/ Greg Shed
  Squanto and the Miracle of Thanksgiving by Eric Metaxas/ Shannon Stirnweis
  Three Young Pilgrims by Cheryl Harness
  Pilgrim's First Thanksgiving by Ann McGovern/ Elroy Freem
  Give Thanks to the Lord by Karma Wilson/ Amy June Bates
- *Rivka's First Thanksgiving* by Elsa Okon Rael/ Maryann Kovalski
- *The Secret of Saying Thanks* by Douglas Wood/ Gred Shed
- *Peter and the Wolf* by Vladimir Vagin
- *Bear Snores On* by Karma Wilson/ Jane Chapman

95

- *Runaway Dreidel!* by Leslea Newman/ Krysten Brooker
- (Born November 28, 1772) *The Man Who Named the Clouds* by Julie Hannah/ John Holub/ Paige Billin-Frye
- (Born November 29, 1832) *Louisa May & Mr. Thoreau's Flute* by Julie Dunlap & Marybeth Lorbiecki/ Mary Azarian
- (Born November 30, 1835) *American Boy: The Adventures of Mark Twain* by Don Brown
River Boy: The Story of Mark Twain by William Anderson/ Dan Andreasen
- (Born November 30, 1874) *Lucy Maud Montgomery* by Alexandra Wallner
- *The Potato Man* by Megan McDonald/ Ted Lewin
- _____
- _____
- _____

(Art) *Through Georgia's Eyes* by Rachel Victoria Rodriquez/ Julie Paschkis and *My Name is Georgia* by Jeanette Winter
(Music) *Music for the End of Time* by Jennifer Bryant/ Beth Peck and *Grateful: A Song of Giving Thanks* by John Bucchino/ Anna-Liisa Hakkarainen
(Poetry) (Published November 10, 1855) *Hiawatha* by Longfellow/ Susan Jeffers
(Language Arts) *The Girl's Like Spaghetti (Apostrophes)* by Lynne Truss/ Bonnie Timmons
(Science/Nature) *Theodoric's Rainbow* by Stephen P. Kramer/ Daniel Mark Duffy
(Shakespeare) *The Tempest* by Marianna Mayer/ Lynn Bywaters
(Math) *Sir Cumference and the Dragon of Pi* by Cindy Neuschwander/ Wayne Geehan and *Sir Cumference and*

the Great Knight of Angleland by Cindy Neuschwander/ Wayne Geehan

(Geography) *Anno's USA* by Mitsumasa Anno and *A is for America* by Devin Scillian/ Pam Carroll

(Fairy Tale) *The Twelve Dancing Princesses* by Marianna Mayers/ K.Y. Craft and *Baba Yaga and Vasilisa the Brave* by Marianna Mayer/ K.Y. Craft

(Myth) *Pegasus* by Marianna Mayer/ K.Y. Craft and *Pegasus, the Flying Horse* by Jane Yolen/ Li Ming

(Tall Tale) *Davy Crockett Saves the World* by Rosalyn Schanzer

---

Notes:

_____

_____

_____

_____

DECEMBER

- (Incident Happened December 1, 1955) *Rosa* by Nikki Biovanni/ Bryan Collier
- (Ship Found December 4, 1872) *Dearest Grandmama* by Catherine Brighton
- (December 6 Feast Day) *The Miracle of Saint Nicholas* by Gloria Whelan/ Judith Brown
- (Event December 7, 1941) *Pearl Harbor* by Stephen Krensky/ Larry Day
- (Born December 10, 1830) *Emily* by Michael Bedard/ Barbara Cooney
  Emily Dickinson's Letters to the World by Jeanette Winter
- *Gingerbread Baby* by Jan Brett
- (December 12, 1531) *The Lady of Guadalupe* by Tomie dePaola
- (Event December 12, 1848) *The Daring Escape of Ellen Craft* by Cathy Moore/ Mary O'Keefe Young
- (Birth Unknown/ Died December 15, 1890) *A Boy Called Slow* by Joseph Bruchac/ Rocco Baviera
- (Born December 17, 1770) *Beethoven Lives Upstairs* by Barbara Nichol/ Scott Cameron
- (Event December 17, 1903) *My Brother's Flying Machine* by Jane Yolen/ Jim Burke

- *An Early American Christmas* by Tomie dePaola
- (Event December 18, 1773) *The Boston Tea Party* by Steven Kroll/ Peter Fiore (or) *Boston Tea Party* by Pamela Duncan Edwards/ Henry Cole
- *The Night Before Christmas* by Clement C. Moore/ Tasha Tudor
- *The Elves and the Shoemaker* by Brothers Grimm/ Jim LaMarche
- *Moishe's Miracle* by Laura Krauss Melmed/ David Slonim
- *Latkes and Applesauce* by Fran Manushkin/ Robin Spowart
- *Too Many Tamales* by Gary Soto/ Ed Martinez
- *Christmas Soup* by Alice Faye Duncan/ Phyllis Dooley/ Jan Spivey Gilchrist
- (Event December 21, 1848) *The Daring Escape of Ellen Craft* by Cathy Moore/ Mary O'Keefe Young
- (Born December 22, 1935) *Tomas and the Library Lady* by Pat Mora/ Raul Colon
- (Born December 23, 1790) *Seeker of Knowledge* by James Rumford
- (Born December 24, 1809) *A Right Fine Life ~ Kit Carson* by Andrew Glass
- (Event December 25, 1776) *When Washington Crossed the Delaware* by Lynne Cheney/ Peter M. Fiore
- (Born December 27, 1822) *Louis Pasteur* by Carol Greene
- _____
- _____
- _____

(Art) *Talking with Tebe': Clementine Hunter, Memory Artist* by Mary E. Lyons

(Music) (December 24, 1818) *Silent Night: The Song and its Story* by Margaret Hodges/ Tim Ladwig
(Poetry) *Silent Night* by Joseph Mohr/ Susan Jeffers and *Christmas Trees* by Robert Frost/ Ted Rand
(Language Arts) *Behind the Mask: A Book about Prepositions* by Ruth Heller
(Science/Nature) *Crinkleroot's Guide to Knowing Animal Habitats* by Jim Arnosky
(Shakespeare) *Winter Song* by William Shakespeare/ Melanie Hall
(Math) *Anno's Mysterious Multiplying Jar* and *Anno's Magic Seeds* by Mitsumasa Anno
(Geography) *Anno's Journey* by Mitsumasa Anno and *Traveling Man (Journey of Ibn Battuta 1325-1354)* by James Rumford
(Fairy Tale) *The Golden Heart of Winter* by Marilyn Singer/ Robert Rayevsky and *Little Red Riding Hood* by Trina Schart Hyman
(Myth) *King Midas and the Golden Touch* by Charlotte Craft/ K.Y. Craft
(Tall Tale) *The Talking Eggs* by Robert D. San Souci/ Jerry Pinkney

Notes:

_____

_____

_____

_____

_____

Following the Pied Piper through History

My father, a reflective, well-educated man, had an insightful opinion about reading the other day. He thinks the reason people aren't reading good literature nowadays isn't because they don't *want* to read; it's because they have *too much* to read.

On a daily basis we have emails to read, memos to read, reports to read, text messages to read, instructions to read. We read the newspaper every morning. We read the stock report on television. We read the magazine headlines at the supermarket check-out aisle. Our children have emails to read, essays to read, textbooks to read, assigned classroom reading. Our culture is in information overload and is being saturated with being told what to read. Few people are allowed to read what they actually want to read and, sadder still, fewer people *care* what they read.

So how do we get our young people (and ourselves) to *care* about what we read? And, even broader, how do we use picture books to get our children to care about events that happened in history and see how they pertain to them and their modern lifestyle. This is a small example but perhaps it will help readers to rethink the way they look at literature and its impact in our lives: past, present and future.

I trust my readers are familiar with the old nursery tale *The Pied Piper of Hamelin*. The above painting is the oldest known picture of the Pied Piper of Hamelin, a replica of the stained glass window placed in the Church of Hamelin in Germany.

The tale of the Pied Piper of Hamelin was recorded by the Brothers Grimm in a fairy tale version and by Robert Browning as a poem. Various dates of the actual event are recorded; Brownings' poem has it recorded on July 22, 1376. Jim Latimer's version *The Irish Piper* has it happening June 16, 1284. The date listed in *The Children's Hour* booklist (June 26, 1284) within this book is taken from Wikipedia. More information about *The Pied Piper of Hamelin* can be found at this website: http://en.wikipedia.org/wiki/The_Pied_Piper_of_Hamelin. The illustrated version of Kate Greenaway's can be found in full text here: http://www.indiana.edu/~librcsd/etext/piper/

I read the poem to my children one autumn day and it left my children's imagination with more questions than I could answer. Their imagination in turn took flight and it would not do except for me to find the answers to their questions.

What happened to the children? Where had they gone? Did their parents find them?

And the ultimate question of all: Did the story really happen?

Because my children cared, I cared. I began to research the story and found (to my amazement) that the story really did happen. Long ago, in the German town of Hamelin, there was a Pied Piper who rid the town of rats and, when denied his payment, lured the children down the streets and to this day the whereabouts of the children are unknown.

"...the Piper turned from the High Street
To where the Weser rolled its waters
Right in the way of their sons and daughters!
However he turned from South to West,
And to Koppelberg Hill his steps addressed,
And after him the children pressed;
Great was the joy in every breast.
``He never can cross that mighty top!
``He's forced to let the piping drop,
``And we shall see our children stop!''
When, lo, as they reached the mountain-side,
A wondrous portal opened wide,
As if a cavern was suddenly hollowed;
And the Piper advanced and the children followed,
And when all were in to the very last,
The door in the mountain-side shut fast."

We heard the Piper's song and followed it. Our research took us down other streets and towns where we explored the countryside of Europe during the Black Plague which spread close on the heels of the Pied Piper. Since the Pied Piper was hired to rid the town of rats, perhaps the town was infested with the plague and many children became unnumbered victims. In the style of old folklore, perhaps the story recorded by the Brothers Grimm was a way to memorialize the loss of all these children. We walked down streets and observed life and clothing styles of this time period. We discussed the Crusades and the timetable between the story

103

and Marco Polo's acquaintance with the Far East. Perhaps the story was told to warn children never to speak, much less follow, strangers who bid them such favors as candy, lost puppies, or:

> "...all the pleasant sights they see,
> ``Which the Piper also promised me.
> ``Where waters gushed and fruit-trees grew,
> ``And flowers put forth a fairer hue,
> ``And everything was strange and new;
> ``The sparrows were brighter than peacocks here,
> ``And their dogs outran our fallow deer,
> ``And honey-bees had lost their stings,
> ``And horses were born with eagles' wings;

We read several versions of the Pied Piper of Hamelin. We compared and contrasted the endings of each. It was a hands-down vote that the favorite version was the one in which the Pied Piper returns the children to their parents and everyone lives happily ever after. We voted for our favorite illustrator. We discussed the different scenarios and told which we preferred and why. We prayed for kidnapped and lost children. We wrote our own endings to the story, all of which ended with the children being returned joyfully to their happy parents.

One of my daughters noted several reference to the Pied Piper in her other readings. She saw the Pied Piper's name in the book *Misty of Chincoteague* by Marguerite Henry and saw it used as the foreshadowing in Lucy Maud Montgomery's *Rainbow Valley* and *Rilla of Ingleside*. She was able to make a connection in these higher levels of reading because of a connection that was sparked from a picture book.

Picture books dovetail nicely with the technological age we're living in. On our attention-deficit days (ie: days overloaded with right information, wrong information, and everybody else's information), they are a refreshing cut-to-the-chase form of information. They are not mangled with boring, useless twaddle or over-our-head hypothesis. Instead, they are clear-cut, to-the-point, personalized sharing and, even better, they make us care about subjects we would otherwise not have been interested in.

Even today my children and I still wonder about the children from the town of Hamelin. We still wonder...and we still care...about the 130 children we never met but who learned and played, sang and danced in the town of Hamelin, Germany.

The Pied Piper of Hamelin by Robert Browning/ Bud Peen
The Pied Piper of Hamelin by Robert Browning/ Kate Greenaway
The Pied Piper of Hamelin by Robert Browning/ Andre Amstutz
The Pied Piper of Hamelin by Robert Browning/ Arthur Rackham
The Pied Piper of Hamelin by Robert Holden/ Drahos Zak
The Pied Piper of Hamelin by Mercer Mayer
The Pied Piper of Hamelin by Diane Suire/ Francesc Rovira

The Pied Piper of Hamelin by Catherine Storr/ Anna Dzierzek

The Pied Piper of Hamelin by Michele Lemieux

The Pied Piper of Hamelin by Deborah Hautzig/ S.D. Schindler

The Irish Piper by Jim Latimer/ John O'Brien

The Pied Piper of Peru by Ann Tompert/ Kestutis Kasparavicius

Educational Services Provided by the Public Library

"...all anyone needs --- is a free public library card and the determination to invest her mind and time in her child's future. The investment can be as small as fifteen minutes a day."
(Trelease, 2001, page. xii, *The Read-Aloud Handbook*)

* * * *

The library is like a huge metropolitan of global economists, brave warriors, boastful lords, inventive scientists, mail-order brides, sullen beggars, homeless orphans, powerful politicians, and other characters vying for our attention to read about them and discover who they are when, all along, we need to be guiding our children to discover who *they* are and what *they* care about.

To discover this, they need to know that a library is a free investment towards their education. In that house of knowledge they will find teachers from every walk of life sitting on the shelves waiting to be taken home. They will also find services that might be the key to opening other doors for them, such as:

♦   Free tutoring

♦   Speeches and readings by published authors

♦   Family reading program

♦   Various musicians demonstrating their instruments

♦   A dance instructor presenting classical and other

        dance demonstrations

- Classes to prepare students for standardized tests
- Workshops to assist taxpayers in filling out their tax forms
- Homework Hotline Assistance
- Genealogy research assistance
- Summertime programs introducing patrons to painting, woodworking, karate, dance, fire safety, drug prevention, stranger danger, wildlife talks, nature study, etc.
- Music Concerts
- How-to/hands-on presentations on candy making, food creations, crafts, and origami
- Story time hour and puppet shows for younger audience
- Access to experts in various fields
- Door-to-door delivery for those confined at home due to infirmity or disability
- Assistance for patrons with cultural and language barriers
- Photocopying
- Hands-on computer classes
- Internet Access
- Job skill preparation and assistance with job interviews and job search

- Job fairs
- Receptive place for book clubs and discussions
- Meeting rooms free of charge
- Picture books inscribed with child's name and date of birth for newborns courtesy of Friends of the Library
- Inter-Library Loan that allows readers to acquire a book from another state
- Writing classes
- Book sales
- Chess club gatherings
- Book parties on the birth date of a famous author/artist hosted by librarians and library workers dressed up as favorite storybook characters
- Newsletter and book reviews of the latest and greatest (and sometimes not so great) book finds
- Gatherings for collectors of coins, stamps, books, etc.
- Assistance with college selection and courses

Picture-Perfect Photo Tip

"You wasted $150,000 on an education you coulda got for a buck fifty in late charges at the public library." ~ Matt Damon's character in *Good Will Hunting*

Literature Pursuit

I love trivia and I think most children do too. There is so much interesting trivia to be found in picture books---if you'll just take a look---and I think it's a great tool to use in getting children interested in what they are reading. There is nothing like a little mystery to spark a feel for adventure and discovery.

Example: Do you know why Trina Schart Hyman's version of *Little Red Riding Hood* offended some readers? If you look closely at the basket Little Red Riding Hood is carrying, you'll see a bottle of whiskey sticking out from under the cloth. It is important to remember, and discuss with your children, that this version of the age-old fairy tale classic was drawn with images of long ago when people used liquor for medicines. Discuss herbs and folk treatment with your child and help them understand that medicine has a long and complex history.

Gone with the Wind by Margaret Mitchell was the number-one bestseller for 40 weeks on the New York Times bestseller's list. Do you know which children's book knocked it off its spot on the bestseller's list? If you thought of *The Story of Ferdinand* by Munro Leaf, you're correct.

Oh, the Places You'll Go! by Dr. Seuss is a book my daughter's French teacher read to the class at the end of their eighth grade year. Her aunt gave the book to her when she graduated from high school (what an appropriate graduation gift) and she reads it every year to remind herself and her class of the places they will go!

Did you know that the story *Rikki-Tikki-Tavi* about a mongoose who saves a family from two deadly cobras and which was made into an animated movie in 1975 was originally written as part of *The Jungle Book*, a book of short stories written by Rudyard Kipling?

Did you know that the story *The Little Red Light House and the Great Gray Bridge* is based on a real-life historical landmark?

Did you know that the story *Roxaboxen* by Alice McLerran is based on the author's fond memories of a make-believe town she and her friends made on a street corner in Arizona?

Did you know that in the original version of the children's classic *Peter Pan* the parents, Mr. and Mrs. Darling, are in fact very poor and have a conversation at the beginning of the book about whether they can afford to keep their children?

Shel Silverstein's small green book *The Giving Tree* was rejected multiple times and one editor told him there was no market for a book that was neither a children's or an adult's book. The book has sold over two million copies and continues to be Silverstein's best known work.

Do you remember the story of *Little Black Sambo*? I can never pour melted butter over hot pancakes without thinking of *Little Black Sambo* and the melted tigers. This book was banned and taken out of print because many black people were offended by the depiction of Little Black Sambo. But I agree with this quote by one reviewer, "If you want to read anything into this story it should be how a little boy outwitted four tigers." This was the storyline that I walked away with upon hearing it for the first time. I thought Little Black Sambo was a brilliant little boy! Surprisingly enough, two black men were the ones who brought this little storybook out of the burn pile and back into our libraries. Julius Lester and Jerry Pinkney have brought this story back to life in a fun, colorful book *Sam and the Tigers* that strives to elevate the original version while keeping the story's originality and mythical storytelling. The author admits to wanting the original *Little Black Sambo* "thrown in the garbage"; yet honestly comments that "...what other story had I read at age seven and remembered for fifty years?" Now *that* is a Living Book! Instead of turning their backs on this classic, they revived it! They paired together and used their talents to add dignity and color to this small masterpiece.

What other trivia finds can you and your children discover in the tomes of picture books?

Enter the *Le Musée des Enfants*

A Picture is Worth a Thousand Words

Children's publishing has much to offer today.

Imagine that you are entering the Metropolitan Museum of Art. Leave behind an exhausting, worried world and enter a peaceful galley of illustrated books. Instead of Leonardo daVinci, Claude Monet, Pablo Picasso, El Greco, and Pierre-Auguste Renoir, we see Tomie dePaola, E.B. Lewis, Beatrix Potter, Patricia Polacco, Jan Brett, Tasha Tudor and Kinuko Y. Craft. The art exhibit is *Le Musée des Enfants* (The Children's Museum).

They say a picture is worth a thousand words; it's no small coincidence that picture books generally consist of only 1000 words. The pictures paint the rest of the story and some authors and artists have taken this knowledge and created genuine masterpieces.

Children's illustrator E.B. Lewis came to our local library in 2006 to talk about his drawing career and how he came to illustrate award-winning children books such as: *The Bat Boy and His Violin, The Other Side,* and *I Love My Hair!* He shared with us how he desired to become a *serious* artist and, when a children's book publisher phoned and asked him to illustrate a picture book, Lewis turned him down. His childhood memory of picture books was not what he considered great, serious art work. So the publisher suggested that he look into some of the newer children books that were being published. Look Lewis did and, what he saw impressed him. He called the publisher back, accepted the assignment, and has been illustrating picture books ever since. He has since blessed families with over 34 illustrated works which, as quoted on his website (www.eblewis.com), he personally selects from manuscripts that show "strong human interest stories ...The kind that evoke emotions...Stories that touch the heart." He illustrates books that "...deal with very tough situations; issues of death and loss and love and friendship." From a serious artist who thought picture books were beneath him to a celebrated children's artist, E. B. Lewis now believes: "Some of the best artwork in the country is being done in children's books." That's high praise indeed.

In an attempt to cut costs and leave more time for preparing students for standardized tests, schools have begun letting go of art as part of the curriculum. What a shame. Education is being ticked off and measured in statistics and percentages, leaving art and personal learning in the dust. Do we attempt to cover over the artist with a mask painted to the expectations of others? Or do we allow our children to listen to the artist inside them?

First we need to ask ourselves, does art matter? If it does, why?

Good quality, wonderfully illustrated picture books with thought-provoking text put the palette of art in the hands of the parents and people who truly care about the child. We can use those palettes to paint our children's hearts.

Whether you are five or fifty, parenting babies or grandbabies, I invite you to take fifteen minutes of your day to explore a new art form with these children and, in doing so, enhance your imagination and your education with no stress, no tests, no instructor, and no expectations except the sheer enjoyment of it.

Art is the blossom that uncoils and blooms despite the earthen crust that unyieldingly conceals and presses it dormant. Art will come forth no matter what tries to bury it because we are all creative beings. Art is what makes the toil of this life possible. Every person desires to leave a little art behind. It might not be some huge architectural feat or some beautiful piece of writing. It might just be some keepsake photo or painting, a simple notation inside our journal, or some small embroidered needle craft; but it is art to the creator. It is in creating something we care about and leaving it to those we love and who love us, that makes it art.

Remove the mask. Remove all expectations of others, enter *Le Musée des Enfants*, and face the exhibit. If not because I say so, then because C.S. Lewis and Jim Trelease say so.

C.S. Lewis:

"No book is really worth reading at age ten which is not
equally worth reading
at the age of fifty."

and

"...a children's story which is only enjoyed by children is a bad children's story."

Jim Trelease (Pages 90-92 of *The Read-Aloud Handbook*):

"A good story is a good story. Beautiful and stirring pictures can move fifteen-year-olds as well as five-year-olds. A picture book(s) should be someplace on the reading list of every class at every level."

Author Fiesta

The ultimate goal of this Author Fiesta is to introduce our children, and ourselves, to various authors and artists who have made it their quest to bring talent into the world of youth and make childhood more meaningful and richer and beautiful than ever before.

By reading illustrated books, you are taking a trip down memory lane with your child beside you. Children authors (and illustrators) have blessed our journey down childhood's roads with their talent in sharing rainy days, fun days, sick days, lost puppy days, picnic days, and holidays. Every child should read these authors and have a personal relationship with his/her pieces of art.

Enter this real life museum of children authors/artists to better familiarize yourself and your child with the creative muses who stir our souls, expand our hearts, and stretch our imaginations.

To all the masters who paint hope and write dreams on the hearts and souls of our children...Thanks for the memories.

The Never-Ending List of Children Authors and Illustrators

(To Read before Your 100th Birthday)

1. David A. Adler (*A Picture Book of Sacagawea*)
2. Allan Ahlberg (*Mockingbird*)
3. Aliki (*A Medieval Feast*)
4. Dan Andreasen (*Rose Red and the Bear Prince*)
5. Kathi Appelt (*Incredible Me!* and *Bat Jamboree*)
6. Cicely Mary Barker (*The Complete Book of the Flower Fairies*)
7. Jill Barklem (*The Secret Staircase* and *Brambly Hedge*)
8. Ludwig Bemelmans (*Madeline*)
9. Barbara Helen Berger (*The Donkey's Dream*)
10. Elsa Beskow (*Around the Year*)
11. Felicia Bond (*If You Give a Pig a Pancake*)
12. Jan Brett (*Annie and the Wild Animals*)
13. Marcia Brown (*Stone Soup*)
14. Margaret Wise Brown (*Goodnight Moon*)
15. Eve Bunting (*Sunflower House*)
16. Robert Burleigh (*Pandora*)
17. Virginia Lee Burton (*The Little House*)
18. Eric Carle (*The Very Hungry Caterpillar*)

19. Nancy White Carlstrom (*Jesse Bear, What will You Wear?*)
20. Jane Chapman (*Mortimer's Christmas Manger*)
21. Raul Colon (*My Mama had a Dancing Heart*)
22. Barbara Cooney (*Miss Rumphius*)
23. Demi (*One Grain of Rice*)
24. Tomie de Paola (*Strega Nona*)
25. Jane Dyer (*Every Year on Your Birthday* and *The Snow Speaks*)
26. Marjorie Flack (*The Story About Ping*)
27. Candace Fleming (*Boxes for Katje*)
28. Mem Fox (*Feathers and Fools*)
29. Paul Galdone (*The Magic Porridge Pot* and *The Teeny-Tiny Woman*)
30. Jean Craighead George (*The First Thanksgiving*)
31. Gail Gibbons (*The Honey Makers*)
32. Diane Goode (*The Most Perfect Spot*)
33. Renee Graef (*Santa Comes to the Little House*)
34. Johnny Gruelle (*Raggedy Ann and Andy stories*)
35. Michael Hague (*The Teddy Bears' Picnic*)
36. Cheryl Harness (*Three Young Pilgrims*)
37. Ruth Heller (*Many Luscious Lollipops*)
38. Russell and Lillian Hoban (*Bread and Jam for Frances*)
39. Deborah Hopkinson (*Bluebird Summer*)
40. Shirley Hughes (*Dogger*)
41. Trina Schart Hyman (*A Child's Calendar*)
42. Susan Jeffers (*My Pony*)
43. Virginia Kahl (*Plum Pudding for Christmas* and *The Duchess Bakes a Cake*)
44. Verla Kay (*Gold Fever* and *Tattered Sails*)
45. Ezra Jack Keats (*Pet Show!* and *Dreams*)
46. Steven Kellogg (*Paul Bunyan*)
47. Jim Lamarche (*The Raft*)
48. John Langstaff (*Frog Went a-courtin'*)
49. Munro Leaf (*The Story of Ferdinand*)

50. Julius Lester (*Sam and the Tigers*)
51. Ted Lewin (*One Green Apple*)
52. E.B. Lewis (*I Love My Hair!* and *Circle Unbroken*)
53. Kim Lewis (*One Summer Day*)
54. Anita Lobel (*Potatoes! Potatoes!* and *On Market Street*)
55. Arnold Lobel (*Frog and Toad stories*)
56. Thomas Locker (*Family Farm*)
57. Marybeth Lorbiecki (*Sister Anne's Hands*)
58. Max Lucado (*The Crippled Lamb*)
59. Patricia MacLachlan (*All the Places to Love*)
60. James Marshall (*Miss Nelson is Missing*)
61. Robert McCloskey (*Blueberries for Sal*)
62. Emily Arnold McCully (*Mirette on the High Wire*)
63. Gerald McDermott (*Musicians of the Sun*)
64. Ann McGovern (*The Lady in the Box*)
65. Patricia McKissack (*Mirandy and Brother Wind*)
66. Lauren A. Mills (*The Goblin Baby*)
67. A. A. Milne (*Winnie the Pooh* and *The Magic Hill*)
68. Josephine Nobisso (*The Weight of a Mass*)
69. Laura Numeroff (*If You Give a Mouse a Cookie*)
70. Jerry Pinkney (*The Nightingale*)
71. Patricia Polacco (*An Orange for Frankie*)
72. Leo Politi (*The Song of the Swallows*)
73. Beatrix Potter (*Peter Rabbit*)
74. Marjorie Priceman (*How to Make an Apple Pie and See the World*)
75. Gloria and Ted Rand (*Sailing Home*)
76. Margot Theis Raven (*America's White Table*)
77. Cynthia Rylant (*The Old Woman Who Named Things*)
78. Robert D. San Souci (*The Talking Eggs*)
79. Allen Say (*Tea with Milk* and *Grandfather's Journey*)
80. Maurice Sendak (*Where the Wild Things Are*)
81. Dr. Seuss (*The Cat in the Hat*)
82. Shel Silverstein (*The Giving Tree*)
83. Peter Spier (*The Stars Spangled Banner*)

84. Eileen Spinelli (*Sophie's Masterpiece: A Spider's Tale*)
85. Diane Stanley (*Michelangelo*)
86. Robert Louis Stevenson (*A Child's Garden of Verses*)
87. Sarah Stewart (*The Gardener*)
88. Ann Tompert (*Grandfather Tang's Story*)
89. Tasha Tudor (*A Time to Keep*)
90. Rosemary Wells (*Waiting for the Evening Star*)
91. Nadine Bernard Westcott (*Skip to my Lou* and *The Lady with the Alligator Purse*)
92. Gloria Whelan (*The Miracle of Saint Nicholas*)
93. Eloise Wilkin (*Mother Goose*)
94. Garth Williams (*Wait Till the Moon is Full*)
95. Karma Wilson (*Bear Snores On*)
96. Audrey and Don Wood (*The Napping House*)
97. Jane Yolen (*Owl Moon*)
98. Paul O. Zelinsky (*Swamp Angel*)
99. Harriet Ziefert (*A New Coat for Anna*)
100. Charlotte Zolotow (*I Like to be Little*)

Authors/Illustrators I Enjoy:

_____

_____

_____

* There are wonderful children authors who are not listed here such as Lucy Maud Montgomery, Lewis Carroll, J.R.R. Tolkien, C.S. Lewis, Laura Ingalls Wilder, Roald Dahl, E.B. White, Maud Hart Lovelace, and many others. My reason for not listing these giants of children's literature is because this list is committed to focusing on *picture book* authors and illustrators. This does not diminish the greater landscape these artists have painted for us. I am always eager to hear which authors and illustrators you enjoy and why. Visit my weblog http://caygibson.typepad.com and email me your suggestions.

Teaching Virtues through Books

Children are born into a world of vices and virtues but they've always had Jiminy Cricket to guide their conscience, the Brothers Grimm to guide their imagination, and Hans Christian Andersen to guide their heart. Right was right and wrong was wrong and never the twine shall meet. Today we live in a land of gray fog and lost childhoods. Jiminy Cricket has been silenced. The Brothers Grimm have been locked away. Hans has been buried. Where do we go to avoid the vices that propel us downward and to uncover the virutes that lift us up?

Sometimes the best rule of thumb involves looking at a simple child's board game to help clarify the rules and redirect our path. I was delighted to find this guide in the classic board game *Chutes and Ladders* (also known by some as *Snakes and Ladders*). What began as a Hindu teaching tool in India was conformed into a Christian "game of morality" once it was introduced in England in 1892. In his April 2006 article *Vice or Virtue?* (authorsden.com), author Tim Philips writes "The game was used to teach children about religion."

Today's modern edition with its cute little boys and girls whizzing down slides and balancing on ladders bears little resemblance to that ancient game; yet the little girl suffering a stomachache and the discarded box of chocolates is proof that the game of vice versus virtues is still as relevant as it was eight-hundred years ago. The end result of both versions is the same. There is a prize at stake and everyone is headed in that direction. In the game of life, vices are the pitfalls, snakes, and chutes that pull us away from the prize. Virtues are the rules we need to follow in order to climb the ladder to attain our reward.

Let's take a peek inside the game box to look at a few of the rule books that can help our children move forward in the game of life:

Compassion:

- *A Song for Lena* by Hilary Horder Hippely is a beautifully illustrated book that sings a song of compassion.
- *The Little Match Girl* by Hans Christian Andersen cannot be overlooked.
- *The Three Questions* is a story originated by Leo Tolstoy and brought back to life by Jon J. Muth
- *Under the Lemon Moon* by Edith Hope Fine will help children to see why it is good to help those who are less fortunate.

Kindness/Generosity/Self-Sacrifice:

- What child cannot be moved to perform a gesture of kindness after reading Shirley Hughes' *Dogger*?
- The gift of self is poignantly shown in *The Gift of the Magi* by O. Henry and will speak generously to older readers.
- *The Magic in You* by Sally H. Taylor
- *Little Rose of Sharon* by Nan Gurley/ Tim Jonke

Diligence/Perseverance:

- Does your young child need to work on diligence and perseverance, as well as, her cooking? *Fannie in the Kitchen* by Deborah Hopkinson is a delicious way of teaching these virtues.
- *The Little Engine that Could* by Watty Piper, of course.

Cheerful Heart/Contentment: Doesn't everyone enjoy a person who has a cheerful heart?

- My all time favorite book is *The Country Bunny and the Little Gold Shoes* by DuBose Heyward. This childhood classic centers on a "*wise,* and *kind,* and *swift...*" as well as "the *bravest* of all the bunnies." But the virtue that shines forth in Mother Cottontail is her cheerful heart as she lives her life and serves her family.

- *The Gardener* by Sarah Stewart is a winner in teaching children to have a cheerful heart while working.
- Another book that is a treasure towards teaching contentment is *The Treasure* by Uri Shulevitz. "Sometimes one must travel far to discover what is near."
- *One Smile* by Cindy McKinley/ Mary Gregg Byrne reminds you that a smile can change the world.

Courage/ Fortitude: Every child loves a story steeped in bravery.

- I recommend Margaret Hodges' book *St. George and the Dragon* beautifully illustrated by Trina Schart Hyman. These books do a wonderful job of teaching fortitude that one needs to sustain one's self through life's hardships and sorrows.
- *First Day in Grapes* by L. King Perez/ Robert Casilla
- *There Come a Soldier* by Peggy Mercer/ Ron Mazellan

Purity: Author Jennie Bishop supplies us with two perfect read-alouds for this virtue.

- *The Squire and the Scroll* and *The Princess and the Kiss* are perfect tales of the "rewards of a pure heart" and "God's gift of purity" and should be on every parent/child's must-read list no matter what their age.

Hospitality:

- *Little Cliff and the Porch People* by Clifton L. Taulbert/ E.B. Lewis

Honesty/Truthfulness:

- *The Hard-Times Jar* by Ethel Footman Smothers/ John Holyfield
- *Matilda Who Told Such Dreadful Lies*...by Hilaire Belloc/Posy Simmonds
- The story *Juan Verdadez: The Man who Couldn't Tell a Lie* by Joe Hayes is an excellent stylus for encrypting the code of "thou shalt not lie" onto your child's

character. Your children will literally be rooting for Juan to tell the truth.

Charity:
- *Stone Soup* by Marcia Brown is the first charitable story that comes to mind. This book gives a wonderful lesson in building a sense of community and giving to the least of your brothers and sisters.
- Another masterpiece in every sense of the word is *Sophie's Masterpiece* by Eileen Spinelli. This little storybook should be read every time you talk to your children about helping mothers and their babies.
- *Bagels from Benny* by Aubrey Davis focuses on a small child's desire to thank God and turns it into a lesson for helping others.
- *The Only One Club* by Jane Naliboff/ Jeff Hopkins

Meekness/Humility:
- *The Crippled Lamb* by Max Lucado is a beautiful book that tells about a meek and gentle lamb who finds favor with God.
- *The Selfish Crocodile* by Faustin Charles
- *Sorry* by Jean Van Leeuwen is an eye-opening story about two brothers who refuse to apologize to one another and shows children how silly pride and stubbornness can be.
- A definite keeper is *The Velveteen Rabbit* by Margery Williams.

Obedience/ Responsibility/ Faithfulness:
- *Little Red Riding Hood* retold by Trina Schart Hyman is a good example for showing children there are consequences to their actions. The consequences and lessons are still prevalent today.
- *Blueberries for Sal* by Robert McCloskey is another good one.
- *The Tale of Peter Rabbit* by Beatrix Potter.
- *Peppe the Lamplighter* by Elisa Bartone/ Ted Lewin

- *Adele & Simon* by Barbara McClintock; follow Adele and Simon around Paris as they both learn responsibility for one another and their belongings.

Dare Your Child to Dream:
- *Lily Brown's Paintings* by Angela Johnson/ E.B. Lewis
- *The Gift of Driscoll Lipscomb* by Sara Yamaka/ Joung Un Kim

General Help:
- *9 Fruits Alive!* by Mindy MacDonald
- *God's Wisdom for Little Girls* by Elizabeth George
- *God's Wisdom for Little Boys* by Jim and Elizabeth George
- *Cookies: Bite-Size Life Lessons* by Amy Krouse Rosenthal and Jane Dyer
- *Is There Really a Human Race?* by Jamie Lee Curtis and Laura Cornell
- *So Few of Me* by Peter H. Reynolds

Life is complicated enough without us having to fudge our way through it. Through a roll of the dice and a play on words, our children are allowed to turn pages that confront vices versus virtues before they actually confront them in real life. The books are manuals that guide them through the game and keep them from sliding too far back as they climb the slippery slope towards the heavenly goal.

Parents might also be interested in checking their libraries for a copy of William Bennett's *Book of Virtues* as well as Karen Santorum's book *Everyday Graces: A Child's Book of Manners*.

Planting the Seeds for Reading

Children of yesteryear lived in gardens---literally and figuratively. Today those gardens look withered and forsaken; but there is a garden of seeds waiting to be sown if only adults would take the thyme (as little as a handful of fifteen-minutes) and step into the garden of time with a child. These seeds promise color and life. They promise a rebirth of the spirit, the soul, and the heart.

Opening a picture book is like opening a packet of seeds. To plant these seed, an adult must enter a child's world and read to a mind that is a ripe receptacle---well-nourished and full of sunshine---ready to receive the fruits.

The A, B, Seeds of Reading

A --- *Annie and the Old One* by Miska Miles

B --- *Bagels from Benny* by Aubrey Davis

C --- *Carla's Sandwich* by Debbie Herman

D --- *Dreams* by Ezra Jack Keats

E --- *Erandi's Braids* by Antonio Hernandez Madrigal

F --- *Feathers and Fools* by Mem Fox

G --- *Gandhi* by Demi

H --- *Horton Hears a Who* by Dr. Seuss

I --- *Island Boy* by Barbara Cooney

J --- *Jubilee* by Ellen Yeomans

K --- *The Kitchen Knight* by Margaret Hodges

L --- *Lu and the Swamp Ghost* by James Carville

M --- *Mike Mulligan and His Steam Shovel* by Virgina Lee Burton

N --- *Nora's Castle* by Satami Ichikawa

O --- *Ox-Cart Man* by Donald Hall

P --- *Peppe the Lamplighter* by Elisa Bartone/ Ted Lewin

Q --- *The Quilting Bee* by Gail Gibbons

R --- *Roxaboxen* by Alice McLerran

S --- *The Selfish Crocodile* by Faustin Charles

T --- *Time of Wonder* by Robert McCloskey

U--- *Uncle Rain Cloud* by Tony Johnston/ Fabricio VandenBroeck

V --- *The Velveteen Rabbit* by Margery Williams

W --- *What You Know First* by Patricia Maclachlan

X --- **Let me know if you find one!**

Y --- *This Year's Garden* by Cynthia Rylant/ Mary Szilagyi

Z --- *Zara's Hats* by Paul Meisel

Picture-Perfect Photo Tip

"A man should hear a little music, read a little poetry, and see a fine picture everyday of
his life, in order that worldly cares may not obliterate the sense of the beautiful which
God has implanted in the human soul."

~ Johann Wolfgang von Goethe ~

Notations of a Mother's Heart

Just as there is time for parties and family gatherings and laughter, there is also a time that we are called, instructed even, to "Be Still!" (Psalm 46:10) While there are several poetic and regal verses in the Bible that speaks more articulately, this one, in its simplicity, is my favorite. I have come back to it more times than I can count. When I'm frazzled, over-extended, over-taxed, and nervous; this small phrase helps calm me. God commands me to *"Be Still!"* and *"Know That I Am God."* He is in control.

There are health benefits related to relaxing with books. Therapists are even prescribing reading lists for their patients. Jo Haslam, a bibliotherapist, says, "Because just about everyone reads, it has been overlooked as a form of therapy. It (reading) can lift people's spirits, help them to resolve problems and, because it requires a deep level of concentration, gets them out of themselves." I think quiet reading time is probably the most relaxing and beneficial (intellectually, mentally, emotionally, and spiritually) stress-reliever...second only to watching fish swim around a fish tank.

Books are friends and reading is a worthy hobby. I have taken great comfort in the books I have read. To realize the full extent that literature plays in our society, listen carefully to Paul Simon's *The Sound of Silence*.

God uses writers every day as an instrument. We are his tools and it is our job to sanctify our time and words and offer it up for His greater glory. So should parents take the finished book as a tool and use it to sanctify our children's lives.

Literature is found not only on library shelves. Literature has taken form and root all the way from Neanderthal caves to Egyptian tombs. There is nothing as exciting for mankind as the discovery of ancient writing that tells who the people were, how they existed, and what they believed. Literature has been found in Jewish cellar walls and Nazi concentration camps. It is found in the strands of Christmas carols and the pamphlets of a neonatal unit. It is found in the diaries of Southern belles who lost husbands and beaux in the Civil War. It is found in your teenage daughter's journal as well as that of a young Jewish girl named Anne Frank who wrote one while in hiding in an attic during World War II. It is found in the spiritual devotional readings that astronaut Rick Husband left behind for his children. It is found in poems written by teenaged girls and found in letters from soldiers in the Middle East written to their families. This captivating song was inspired by words found inscribed on the walls of a cellar in Cologne, Germany, where Jews were in hiding:

"I believe in the sun, even when it isn't shining.
I believe in love, even when there's no one there.
And I believe in God, even when He is silent.

"I believe in miracles,
I believe in love,
I believe that there can always be a way.
I believe that He is calling us,
I believe that He is calling us;
that all things are possible with God."

Literature is alive all around us. It is found in the ideas, the inspiration, the heart and soul of life which are often printed, bound and nicely tucked between two covers of a book for future generations and for the sake of posterity. It is up to us to turn it into something good and beautiful.

Thornton Wilder, in *The Bridge of San Luis Rey*, empowers this when referencing one character's reception of letters from another character, "*...he had extracted all their richness and the intention, missing (as most readers do) the whole purport of literature, which is the notation of the heart.*"

There is the immediate answer. Literature is the notation of the heart. There is an example of this in the Civil War-era movie, *Cold Mountain* starring Nicole Kidman and Renee Zellweger. The two women characters portrayed by Nicole and Renee are building a fence, trying to do a man's work of repairs around the farm. Nicole begins lamenting that this is the first constructive thing she's ever done in her life. Before the war, she only knew French and hand-embroidery and piano, but this was the first thing she has ever done that made a difference. The other accomplishments of her life no longer matter in the culture-of-war she now lives in.

For some reason that gave me pause. What have I done in my lifetime that has made a difference? And what is it about patching a fence on a farm that is more constructive than speaking French, embroidering a picture, or playing the piano? Does patching a fence with one's hands have more substance than playing the piano with one's hands? Does having a career and prestige have more substance than the work one does within the home and the imprint left upon one's child?

Classical education fell out of favor in America during the impoverished days of the Civil War. Suddenly a classical education no longer mattered. Art didn't feed a hungry baby. Poetry did not feed a houseful of people. Speaking French did not stop the carpetbaggers from taking over your farm. Embroidering a shirt did not matter if there were no shoes to wear through the winter.

Families needed hands that knew how to work a farm. They needed hands that knew how to sew a dress out of a curtain and make new harnesses. They needed minds that could bargain for supplies. They needed strong backs that could plow a field, repair a fence, plant a garden, or work a trade. They needed sharp minds that could alter figures so the carpetbaggers could not make claim to the family farm. Classics and liberal arts held nothing for the common man. Nothing at all except perhaps, memories and dreams that were *gone with the wind.*

Yet there is a redemptive scene in *Cold Mountain* immediately following the farm scene: it is night and only the candles near the piano burns. Nicole's character is playing a beautiful piece on the ivories and Renee's character (a harsh, hillbilly, redneck of a woman) is silently witnessing the melody from the recesses of the stairwell. Silently, and ever so gently, she begins to sway back-and-forth, back-and-forth. She closes her eyes and continues to sway as the music plays on. The moment is solemn; the moment brings calm to the troubled heart and peace to the troubled soul. As rough as Renee's character is, a burr falls away. A soul is laid bare. A notation is made upon the heart.

The achieved moment brings hope for a better tomorrow. Hands can be used to mend fences and feed our families. Hands can also be used to write beauty on the souls of our families. Ultimately, literature is simply putting into words what touches our hearts and minds.

Literature, whether through art, music, books, etc. is always the notation of one heart to another. Always. I commit myself once again to teaching my children from good literature on a daily basis. Books really must be lived. Some books do this very effectively, drawing the reader into a kingdom far, far away. Other times the visuals and hands-on experience are necessary. Real living teaches us things that books cannot, but it is the books and the wisdom of the years that teaches us why the living is so important and what we are living for.

Literature is the way we educate, the way we live, the way we breathe. It is always a notation of our heart.

Going home after dropping some little friends off, I stopped briefly at the library to return some books. My young daughter was looking at her library card and asked, "Mom, am I lucky to have this card?"

"You sure are," I told her. "In your hand you hold the power to be as smart as you want to be and as smart as God wants you to be." The weapon of empowerment and

133

endearment is in her hands and a notation is left upon her heart.

Petit Fours for Mom

This section is dedicated to mothers (and grandmothers) because often they are the ones who leave the first notations upon our hearts and who plant the first seeds of rhyme and prose in our ears. To empower and endear our children's heart and make them receptive to these seeds, we must first implant them into our own.

I am a collector of illustrated books. I don't see silly children's stuff when I look at a well-written, well-illustrated book. Rather, I see emotion and character and ideals and art. I invite you to brew yourself a cup of tea or coffee and gather some of these *petit fours* (picture books) onto a table near your favorite reading spot. Think of them as you do psalm readings and scripture verses. They are the fiber that sustains us during the moments we cannot find the nourishment we need to get us to the next step of daily life. They are the sweet jellies and jams that help us endure the bitter herbs of life.

Think of this as a prescribed reading list for those times you are weary, heart-sick, overwhelmed, and overburden. I hope it renews your spirit, resolves your concerns, relaxes you, and benefits you intellectually, mentally, emotionally, and spiritually.

- ❖ **For stepmothers and foster mothers:** *The Memory String* by Eve Bunting/ Ted Rand---a little girl's family heirloom button-string proves to be the tie that binds her to her new stepmother.
- ❖ **For pregnant mothers worried about caring for their newborn baby:** *Sophie's Masterpiece* by Eileen Spinelli/ Jane Dyer---a lovely book about an artistic spider whose artwork goes unnoticed until the very end when she weaves a baby blanket for a poor mother and her newborn baby.
- ❖ **For adoptive mothers:** *Everytime You Call Me Mommy: An Adoption Blessing* by Kimberly Kane/ Bitsey Crismon---a reflective remembrance for all adoptive mothers to share with the children who call them Mommy.
- ❖ **For new mothers:** *Angel in the Waters* by Regina Doman/ Ben Hatke---perfect for new mothers to read. A wonderful baby shower gift.
- ❖ **For mothers when the baby won't stop crying:** *A Drop of Rain* by Wong Herbert Yee
- ❖ **For stay-at-home moms feeling they have lost their identity:** *The Treasure* by Uri Shulevitz---this book helps you to focus on where your real treasure lies, and it is usually within arm's reach. Also, *The Seeds of Peace* by Laura Berkeley/ Alison Dexter---a wealthy merchant seeks the peace that an old hermit has and desires to learn how to obtain it.
- ❖ **For mothers who work outside the home:** *Coming on Home Soon* by Jacqueline Woodson/ E.B. Lewis---this book is "like a song you want to sing over and over." A mother has to work during wartime and leaves her young daughter with grandma.

- ❖ **For homeless mothers:** *December* by Eve Bunting/David Diaz---in sharing their cardboard box and extra cookie with another homeless person, a homeless mother and her son receive Christmas blessings. Will bring hope and balm to mothers trying to raise children in homeless situations.
- ❖ **For mothers frustrated with the demands of motherhood:** *The Country Bunny and the Little Gold Shoes* by Dubose Heyward/ Marjorie Flack---A country bunny grows up to train her little countries bunnies well and to follow the paths they should go while discovering a path of her own.
- ❖ **Mothers who long for a simpler life and inner peace:** *When I was Young in the Mountains* by Cynthia Rylant/ Diane Goode---a little girl remembers a simpler life growing up in the mountains.
- ❖ **For mothers when their children argue:** *Sorry!* by Jean van Leeuwen/ Brad Sneed---this is a story about two brothers who argue and how their refusal to say "I'm sorry" divides their family for many long years. Good fodder to read alongside one's children.
- ❖ **For mothers dealing with childhood bullying issues:** *Alley Oops* by Janice Levy.
- ❖ **For mothers who love to cook and bake:** *Fannie in the Kitchen* by Deborah Hopkinson/ Nancy Carpenter---a delightful read. Mommies and their little girls will love it. Also, *Miss Opal's Auction* by Susan Vizurraga/ Mark Graham will make every mother want to begin journaling her recipes.
- ❖ **For mothers to read before taking their child shopping with them:** *The Big Green Pocketbook* by Candice F. Ransom/ Felicia Bond---a wonderful tale of a little girl who goes to town with her mother and captures her whole morning inside her big green pocketbook.

- ❖ **For mothers who are too busy:** *Someday: Is Not a Day of the Week* by Denise Brennan-Nelson/ Kevin O'Malley
- ❖ **For mothers to read to a child who feels unloved:** *Just in Case You Ever Wonder* by Max Lucado---wonderful prose to soothe an aching heart.
- ❖ **For mothers showing their child his place is our world:** *Annie and the Old One* by Miska Miles/ Peter Parnall
- ❖ **For mothers as we guide our children:** *I'll Be With You Always* by Joni Eareckson Tada/ Craig Nelson
- ❖ **For mothers who feel their child is out of step with the rest of the world:** *Rocks in His Head* by Carol Otis Hurst/ James Stevenson---a daughter shares the story of her father and his fascination with rocks.
- ❖ **For mothers who are getting remarried and blending families:** *The Ring Bear* by David Michael Slater/ S.G. Brooks
- ❖ **For mothers who feel smothered beneath little hands that need her:** *The Velveteen Rabbit* by Margery Williams---illness, painful moments, and trials come to all of us, but it is because of these times that we rise stronger, more grateful, and more alive than we were before.
- ❖ **For mothers who woke up on the wrong side of the bed this morning:** *Mrs. Biddlebox* by Linda Smith/ Marla Frazee---Join Mrs. Biddlebox has she takes her gray, rotten morning and bakes it into a cake! Read this one with your kids.
- ❖ **For mothers and daughters:** *This Quiet Lady* by Charlotte Zolotow/ Anita Lobel
- ❖ **For mothers and sons:** *Love You Forever* by Robert Munsch/ Sheila McGraw and *Moonlight on the River* by Deborah Kovacs/ William Shattuck
- ❖ **For mothers giving their children wings to fly:** *A Mother's Wish* by Kathy-Jo Wargin/ Irena Roman

- ❖ **For mothers rocking a child:** *On Mother's Lap* by Ann Herbert Scott/ Glo Coalson---to read with your child(ren) and offer reassurance that there is plenty of room in mother's rocking chair as well as her heart.
- ❖ **For mothers who are displeased with a wayward child:** *The Giving Tree* by Shel Silverstein---a classic about a boy and a tree who grow old together.
- ❖ **For mothers wanting to hang on while having to let go:** *Letting Swift River Go* by Jane Yolen/ Barbara Cooney
- ❖ **For mothers during war time:** *Potatoes! Potatoes!* by Anita Lobel
- ❖ **For mothers remembering loved ones who are no longer here:** *The Hundred Penny Box* by Sharon Bell Mathis/ Leo Diane Dillon---a little boy knows that the old battered box contains something more priceless than the pennies inside. Also, *The Patchwork Quilt* by Valerie Flournoy/ Jerry Pinkney.
- ❖ **For mothers having to place their elderly parents in a care center or nursing home:** *Oma's Quilt* by Paulette Bourgeois/ Stephane Jorisch---this book paints a generational picture of a grandmother, daughter, and granddaughter having to bear the winds of change together.
- ❖ **For mothers who are newly grandmothers:** *When Grandma Came* by Jill Paton Walsh/ Sophy Williams
- ❖ **For mothers going on a walk with their children or wanting to show their children the world God gave us:** *All the Places to Love* by Patricia Maclachlan/ Michael Wimmer and *Pobble's Way* by Simon Van Booy/ Wendy Edelson and *Play with Me* by Marie Hall Ets and *Zoe's Tower* by Paul and Emma Rogers/ Robin Bell Corfield.
- ❖ **For mothers who long to plant meaningful seeds in the hearts of their children:** *Miss Rumphius* by

139

Barbara Cooney and *My Great-Aunt Arizona* by Gloria Houston/ Susan Condie Lamb.

❖ **A Psalm for Mothers and Older Children**: *I Will Hold You 'Til You Sleep* by Linda Zuckerman/ Jon J. Muth

❖ **For mothers at Christmastime:** *Mary, Did You Know?* by Mark Lowry---reminding us of the reason for the season. *When it Snowed that Night* by Norma Farber/ Petra Mathers---a lovely poetic book that reminds mothers that Advent is the time to meditate upon the children we are blessed to have at our knees:

I never got to Bethlehem, someone, I thought, should (day and night) be here, someone should stay at home. I think I was probably right.

For I have sung my child to dream far, far away from where there lies a woman doing much the same. And neither of our children cries.

❖ **Must read for all mothers:** *Let Me Hold You Longer* (my personal favorite) by Karen Kingsbury/ Mary Collier.

❖ **For mothers wanting to leave a notation upon their children's hearts**: *What You Know First* by Patricia MacLachlan/ Barry Moser.

Pack Your Suitcase
(and make sure some of these books are packed inside)
Spanning the Globe

Africa
☐ *Bringing the Rain to Kapiti Plain* by Verna Aardema/ Beatriz Vidal

☐ *The Day Gogo Went to Vote* by Elinor Batezat Sisulu/ Sharon Wilson

☐ *Africa is not a Country* by Margy Burns Knight/ Anne Sibley O'Brien

☐ *Galimoto* by Karen Lynn Williams/ Catherine Stock

☐ _____

Asia
☐ *Himalaya* by Tenzing Norbu Lama

☐ *I, Doko: The Tale of a Basket* by Ed Young

☐ _____

Australia
☐ *Are We There Yet?* By Alison Lester

☐ _____

Baghdad
☐ *The Girl Who Lost Her Smile* by Karim Alrawi/ Stefan Czernecki
☐ _____

Canada
☐ *Jeffery and Sloth* by Kari-Lynn Winters/ Ben Hodson
☐ *The Sugaring-Off Party* by Jonathan London/ Gilles Pelletier
☐ *Under a Prairie Sky* by Anne Laurel Carter/ Alan and Lea Daniel
☐ _____

Caribbean Islands
☐ *The Faithful Friend* by Robert D. San Souci/ Brian Pinkney
☐ _____

Chile
☐ *Mia's Story: A Sketchbook of Hopes and Dreams* by Michael Foreman
☐ _____

China
☐ *The Empty Pot* by Demi
☐ *Tikki Tikki Tembo* by Arlene Mosel/ Blair Lent
☐ See complete list under ***Master Booklist***
☐ _____

Czechoslovakia
☐ *The Three Golden Keys* by Peter Sis
☐ _____

Egypt
- [ ] *Gift of the Nile* by Jan M. Mike/ Charles Reasoner
- [ ] _____

England
- [ ] *Chaucer's Canterbury Tales* by Marcia Williams/ Lynn Bywaters
- [ ] _____

Ethiopia
- [ ] *Only a Pigeon* by Jane and Christopher Kurtz/ E.B. Lewis
- [ ] *The Perfect Orange: A Tale from Ethiopia* by Frank P. Araujo/ Hsiao-Chun Li
- [ ] *The Best Beekeeper of Lalibela: A Tale from Africia* by Cristina Kessler/ Leonard Jenkins
- [ ] *Fire on the Mountain* by Jane Kurtz/ E.B. Lewis
- [ ] _____

France
- [ ] *Adele and Simon* by Barbara McClintock
- [ ] *Madeline* by Ludwig Bemelmans
- [ ] _____

Holland
- [ ] *The Boy Who Held Back the Sea* by Mary Mapes Dodge/ Thomas Locker
- [ ] *The Hole in the Dike* by Norma B. Green/ Eric Carle
- [ ] *Katje the Windmill Cat* by Gretchen Woelfle/ Nicola Bayley
- [ ] *Hana in the Time of the Tulips* by Deborah Noyes/ Bagram Ibatoulline
- [ ] _____

India

☐ *Lily's Garden of India* by Jeremy Smith/ Rob Hefferan
☐ *Monsoon* by Uma Krishnaswami/ Jamel Akib
☐ *Taj Mahal* by Caroline Arnold/ Madeleine Comora/ Rahal Bhaghan
☐ _____

Ireland

☐ *Small Beauties* by Elvira Woodruff/ Adam Rex
☐ *Katie's Wish* by Barbara Shook Hazen/ Emily Arnold McCully
☐ _____

Italy

☐ *Strega Nona* by Tomie dePaola
☐ *Papa Piccolo* by Carol Talley/ Itoko Maeno
☐ *Gabriella's Song* by Candace Fleming/ Giselle Poter
☐ _____

Japan

☐ *A Pair of Red Clogs* by Masako Matsuno/ Kazue Mizumura
☐ *Grass Sandals* by Dawnine Spivak/ Demi
☐ *Under the Cherry Blossom Tree, Tree of Cranes,* and other books by Allen Say
☐ _____

Kenya

☐ *Mama Panya's Pancakes: A Village Tale from Kenya* by Mary and Rich Chamberlin/ Julia Cairns
☐ _____

Korea

☐ *The Trip Back Home* by Janet S. Wong/ Bo Jia

☐ _____

Madagascar
☐ *New King* by Doreen Rappaport/ E.B. Lewis
☐ _____

Mexico
☐ *How Music Came to the World* by Hal Ober/ Carol Ober
☐ *Cactus Soup* by Eric A. Kimmel/ Phil Huling
☐ *Erandi's Braids* by Antonio Hernandez Madrigal/ Tomie dePaola
☐ _____

Peru
☐ *The Pied Piper of Peru* by Ann Tompert/ Kestutis Kasparavicius
☐ *Tonight is Carnaval* by Arthur Dorros
☐ _____

Poland
☐ *The Cats in Krasinski Square* by Karen Hesse/ Wendy Watson
☐ _____

Puerto Rica
☐ *Juan Bobo Goes to Work: A Puerto Rican Folk Tale* by Marisa Montes/ Joe Cepeda
☐ *The Golden Flower: A Taino Myth from Puerto Rico* by Nina Jaffe/ Enrique O. Sanchez
☐ *The Legend of the Hummingbird: A Tale from Puerto Rico* by Michael Rose Ramirez/ Margaret Sanfilippo
☐ _____

Russia
☐ *Luba and the Wren* by Patricia Polacco

☐ *The Wolfhound* by Kristine L. Franklin/ Kris Waldherr
☐ *Philipok* by Leo Tolstoy/ Ann Keay Beneduce/ Gennady Spirin
☐ *Sasha's Matrioshka Dolls* by Jana Dillon/ Deborah Lattimore
☐ _____

Spain
☐ *The Beautiful Butterfly: A Folktale from Spain* by Judy Sierra/ Victoria Chess
☐ *The Three Golden Oranges* by Alma Flor Ada/ Reg Cartwright
☐ _____

Tanzania
☐ *My Rows and Piles of Coins* by Tololwa M. Mollel/ E.B. Lewis
☐ _____

Vietnam
☐ *The Lotus Seed* by Sherry Garland/ Tatsuro Kiuchi
☐ _____

Picture-Perfect Photo Tip

Drawing is speaking to the eye; talking is painting to the ear.
~ Joseph Joubert

Read Across America

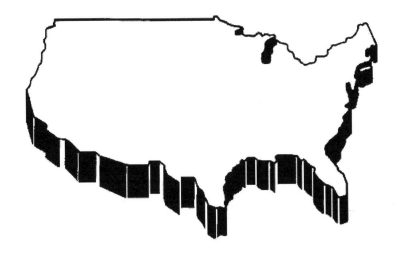

A couple of years ago a friend gifted me with the book *P is for Pelican: A Louisiana Alphabet.* She knew I would love it. Granted, alphabet books are a dime a dozen, but the *Discover America State-by-State Alphabet* series published by Sleeping Bear Press far exceeds the reader's expectations. There is a book per state and within these little book-sized suitcases is a map to state landmarks, historical sites, historical figures, and symbols. There is a rhyming verse on each page that is for old and young alike. After this reading, the younger listeners can either run on to their playtime or sit and enjoy the lovely artwork. Older readers can go further along the trail to additional text which will encourage further learning. These wonderful resources are colorful, appropriate for all ages, and, like a roll of postage stamps, link all the states together.

Explore America with your children and find out where the trail leads you.

Alabama

☐ *A is for Alabama* by E.J. Sullivan

☐ *Wind Flyers* by Angela Johnson

Alaska

☐ *Baby in a Basket* by Gloria Rand/ Ted Rand

☐ *Akiak: A Tale from the Iditarod* by Robert Blake

☐ *Under Alaska's Midnight Sun* by Deb Vanasse

☐ *Raven and River* by Nancy White Carlstrom

Arizona

☐ *Roxaboxen* by Alice McLerran/ Barbara Cooney

☐ *Annie and the Old One* by Miska Miles/ Peter Parnall

☐ *Cactus Hotel* by Brenda Z. Guiberson/ Megan Lloyd

Arkansas

☐ *N is for Natural State: An Arkansas Alphabet* by Michael Shoulders/ Rick Anderson

☐ *Under One Flag* by Liz Parkhurst/ Tom Clifton

California

☐ *Song of the Swallows* by Leo Politi

☐ *Nine for California* by Sonia Levitin/ Cat Bowman Smith

☐ *Earthquake* by Milly Lee/ Yangsook Choi

☐ *Sierra* by Diane Siebert/ Wendell Minor

Colorado

☐ *Roundup at the Palace* by Kathleen Cook Waldron/ Alan & Lea Daniel

☐ *High as a Hawk* by T.A. Barron/ Ted Lewin

Connecticut

☐ *N is for Nutmeg: A Connecticut Alphabet* by Elissa Grodin/ Maureen K. Brookfield

☐ *A Picture Book of Harriet Beecher Stowe* by David Adler

Delaware

☐ *When the Shadbush Blooms* by Carla Messinger/ Susan Katz/ David Kanietakeron Fadden

Florida

☐ *Billy's Search for Florida Undersea Treasure* by Minerva Smiley/ Russ Smiley

☐ *Welcome to the River of Grass* by Jane Yolen/ Laura Regan

☐ *Everglades* by Jean Craighead George/ Wendell Minor

Georgia

☐ *The Waving Girl* by J.B. Nicholas/ Joan C. Waites

Hawaii

☐ *The Last Princess: The story of Princess Ka'iulani of Hawai'i* by Fay Stanley

Idaho

☐ *Mailing May* by Michael O. Tunnell/ Ted Rand

Illinois

☐ *Haystack* by Bonnie and Arthur Geisert

☐ *Growing Seasons* by Elsie Lee Splear/ Ken Stark

Indiana

☐ *The Floating House* by Scott Russell Sanders/ Helen Cogancherry

Iowa

☐ *Kate Shelley and the Midnight Express* by Margaret K. Wetterer/ Karen Ritz

Kansas

☐ *Going West* by Nancy Van Leeuwen

☐ *The Bravest of Us All* by Marsha Diane Arnold/ Brad Sneed

☐ *Climbing Kansas Mountain* by George Shannon/ Thomas B. Allen

Kentucky

☐ *We Played Marbles* by Tres Seymour/ Dan Andreason

Louisiana

☐ *Sweet Magnolias* by Virginia L. Kroll/ Laura Jacques

☐ *Bayou Lullaby* by Kathi Appelt/ Neil Waldman

Maine

☐ *One Morning in Maine* by Robert McClosky

☐ *Time of Wonder* by Robert McClosky

Maryland

☐ *By The Dawn's Early Light* by Steven Kroll

Massachusetts

☐ *Make Way for Ducklings* by Robert McClosky

☐ *Johnny Appleseed* by Steven Kellog

Michigan

☐ *The Legend of Michigan* by Trinka Hakes Noble/ Gijsbert Van Frankenhuyzen

Minnesota

☐ *Up North at the Cabin* by Marsha Wilson Chall/ Steve Johnson

☐ *Storm Codes* by Tracy Nelson Maurer/ Christina Rodriquez

Mississippi

☐ *Freedom Summer* by Deborah Wiles/ Jerome Lagarrigue

Missouri

☐ *S is for Show Me: A Missouri Alphabet* by Judy Young/ Ross B. Young

Montana

☐ *First Dog: Unleashed in the Montana Capitol* by Jessica Solberg/ Robert Rath

Nebraska

☐ *The Schoolchildren's Blizzard* by Marty Rhodes Figley/ Shelly O. Haas

☐ *The Huckabuck Family and How They Raised Popcorn in Nebraska and Quit and Came Back* by Carl Sandburg/ David Small

Nevada

☐ *S is for Silver: A Nevada Alphabet* by Eleanor Coerr/ Darcie Park

☐ *Rhyolite: The True Story of a Ghost Town* by Diane Siebert/ David Frampton

New Hampshire

☐ *Old Home Town* by Donald Hall/ Emily Arnold McCully

☐ *Tuttle's Red Barn* by Richard Michelson/ Mary Azarian

New Jersey

☐ *The Legend of the Cape May Diamond* by Trinka Hakes Noble/ E. B. Lewis

New Mexico

☐ *Manuela's Gift* by Kristyn Rehling Estes/ Claire Cotts

☐ *Farolitos for Abuelo* by Rudolfo Anaya/ Edward Gonzales

New York

☐ *How Pizza Came to Queens* by Dayal Kaur Khalsa

☐ *Tar Beach* by Faith Ringold

☐ *Little Farm by the Sea* by Kay Chorao

☐ *Flying Over Brooklyn* by Myron Uhlberg/ Gerald Fitzgerald

North Carolina

☐ *Wright Brothers* by Russell Freedman

☐ *My Great-Aunt Arizona* by Gloria Houston

☐ *Back Home* by Gloria Jean Pinkney/ Jerry Pinkney

North Dakota

☐ *Dakota Dugout* by Ann Turner/ Ronald Himler

Ohio

☐ *Lentil* by Robert McClosky

☐ *Johnny Appleseed Goes A'Planting* by Patsy Jensen

Oklahoma

☐ *Dancing with the Indians* by Angela Shelf Medearis/ Constance Marshall

☐ *Angels in the Dust* by Margot Theis Raven/ Roger Essley

Oregon

☐ *Apples to Oregon* by Deborah Hopkinson/ Nancy Carpenter

Pennsylvania

☐ *Christmas Cookie Tree* by Ruth Hershey Irion

☐ *The Egg Tree* by Katherine Milhous

☐ *Auntie Anne, My Story* by Anne Beiler/ Freimen Stoltzfus

Rhode Island

☐ *R is for Rhode Island Red: A Rhode Island Alphabet* by Mark R. Allio/ Mary Jane Begin

South Carolina

☐ *A Sweet, Sweet Basket* by Margie Willis Clary/ Dennis L. Brown

☐ *The Mysterious Tail of a Charleston Cat* by Ruth Paterson Chappell/ Bess Paterson Shipe/ Dean Wroth

☐ *Rosebud Roams Charleston* by Sally Smith

South Dakota

☐ *Who Carved the Mountain? The Story of Mount Rushmore* by Jean L.S. Patrick/ Renee Graef

☐ *Moonstick: The Seasons of the Sioux* by Eve Bunting/ John Sandford

Tennessee

☐ *Swamp Angel* by Anne Isaacs

☐ *When the Whippoorwill Calls* by Candice Ransom/ Kimberly Root

☐ *A Band of Angels: a Story Inspired by the Jubilee Singers* by Deborah Hopkinson/ Raul Colon

Texas

☐ *Armadillo Rodeo* by Jan Brett

☐ *The Cotton Candy Catastrophe at the Texas State Fair* by Dotti Enderle/ Chuck Galey

☐ *Legend of the Bluebonnet* by Tomie dePaola

Utah

☐ *Ten Mile Day: The Building of the Transcontinental Railroad* by Mary Ann Fraser

Vermont

☐ *Snowflake Bentley* by Jacqueline Martin

☐ *Waiting for the Evening Star* by Rosemary Wells/ Susan Jeffers

☐ *Daisy and the Doll* by Michael and Angela Medearis/ Larry Johnson

Virginia

☐ *Promise Quilt* by Candice Ransom/ Ellen Beier

☐ *The Relatives Came* by Cynthia Rylant/ Stephen Gammell

Washington

☐ *Baby in a Basket* by Gloria Rand/ Ted Rand

☐ *Love as Strong as Ginger* by Lenore Look/ Stephen T. Johnson

☐ *Salmon Forest* by David Suzuki/ Sheena Lott

West Virginia

☐ *The Rag Coat* by Lauren Mills

☐ *When I was Young in the Mountains* by Cynthia Rylant

Wisconsin

☐ *The Raft* by Jim LaMarche

☐ *Summertime in the Big Woods* by Laura Ingalls Wilder/ Renee Graef

☐ *Winter Days in the Big Woods* by Laura Ingalls Wilder/ Renee Graef

Wyoming

☐ *Legend of the Indian Paintbrush* by Tomie DePaola

Special thanks to Mary Machado for filling in the valleys and crevices of this state-wide booklist.

Let's Get Cooking with Literature
(Compiled for all Zesty Readers)
~ Happy reading and eating! ~

Food! We all love it. Our kids love it. Combine it with books and you've got a sure fire grill of tempting morsels just waiting for you at the library. In this list, as well as this whole book, I want to borrow Rachael Ray's cooking philosophy. These 15-minute literary cookbooks are meant to resemble Rachael Ray's 30-minute dishes. It's "all about simplifying, really good living, accessibility and sharing." Bring the children and get ready to read and cook. Spend time in the kitchen. Spend time with a book. Spend time with your child. Those are the ingredients that make a perfect afternoon of memories.

Here is a twelve month shopping list of books to take to the library and load into your shopping cart. This list will become a delicious treat the whole family can enjoy. It's *book*-a-licious!

☐ *36 Strange Little Animals Waiting to Eat: With Simple Little Recipes to Make* by Graham Percy/ Roz Denny (Various Recipes)

☐ *A Birthday Cake is No Ordinary Cake* by Debra Frasier (The Spinning World Birthday Cake Recipe)

☐ *Cranberry Birthday* by Wende and Harry Devlin (Grandmother's Birthday Cake Recipe)

☐ *The Cookie Store Cat* by Cynthia Rylant (Recipes for Gumdrop Gems, Gingerbread Men, Father Eugene's Scotch Chewies, After-School Bachelor Buttons, Frosty Fruit Squares, Santa Claus Faces, and Cinnamon Sugar Plums)

☐ *Missing May* by Cynthia Rylant (May's Vegetable Soup)

☐ *Olga's Cup and Saucer* by Olga Bravo Five (Recipes appear as the months go by: Strawberry Corn Muffins, A-Z Afternoon Cake, Fresh Raspberry Pizza and others)

☐ *Everything on a Waffle* by Polly Horvath (Older readers---recipes at end of each chapter)

January ~ Gumbos & Soups

☐ *Dumpling Soup* by Jama Kim Rattigan/ Lillian Hsu-Flanders (New Year's Celebration ~ Mandoo Dumplings Recipe)

☐ *Grandpa's Soup* by Eiko Kadono/ Satomi Ichikawa (Soup Recipe)

☐ *Chicken Soup by Heart* by Esther Hershenhorn/ Rosanne Litzinger (Chicken Soup Recipe)

☐ *Four Seasons of Corn: A Winnebago Tradition* by Sally M. Hunter/ Joe Allen (Indian Corn Soup Recipe)

☐ *Growing Vegetable Soup* by Lois Ehlert (Growing Garden Vegetables ~ Vegetable Soup Recipe)

☐ *Gator Gumbo: A Spicy-Hot Tale* by Candace Fleming/ Sally Anne Lambert (Maman's Spicy-Hot Gumbo Recipe)

☐ *Grandma's Gumbo* by Deborah Ousley Kadair (Gumbo Recipe)

☐ *The Real Story of Stone Soup* by Ying Chang Compestine (Egg Drop Stone Soup)

☐ *Jolie Blonde and the Three Heberts* by Sheila Hebert Collins/ Patrick Soper (Gumbo Recipe)

☐ *Carrot Soup* by John Segal (Carrot Soup Recipe)

☐ *Making Minestrone* by Stella Blackstone/ Nan Brooks (Magic Minestrone Soup Recipe)

☐ *Cucumber Soup* by Vickie Leigh Krudwig/ Craig McFarland Brown (Cucumber Soup Recipe)

☐ *Stone Soup* by Heather Forest/ Susan Gaber (Stone Soup Recipe)

☐ *Pumpkin Soup* by Helen Cooper (Pumpkin Soup Recipe)

☐ *Pizza Soup* by Fay Robinson/ Ann Iosa (Pizza Soup Recipe)

☐ *Mud Soup* by Judith Head/ Susan Guevara (Mud Soup ~ Black Bean Soup Recipe)

☐ *Matzah Ball Soup* by Joan Rothenberg (Three Variations of Matzah Ball Soup Recipe)

☐ *The Mice of Bistro des Sept Freres* by Marie LeTourneau (Go to author's website for Cheese Soup Recipe ~ *Soup au Fromage* ~ http://www.marieletourneau.com/)

☐ *Sip, Slurp, Soup, Soup, Caldo, Caldo, Caldo* by Diane Gonzales Bertrand/ Alex Pardo Delange (Caldo ~ Soup Recipe)

☐ *Still-Life Stew* by Helena Clare Pittman (Rosa's Still-Life Stew ~ Vegetable Stew Recipe)

☐ *Cactus Soup* by Eric A. Kimmel/ Phil Huling (Cactus-Spine Soup ~ Chili Recipe)

☐ *The Ugly Vegetables* by Grace Lin (Ugly Vegetable Soup Recipe)

☐ *Everybody Serves Soup* by Norah Dooley/ Peter J. Thornton (Cultural Soup Recipes)

☐ *Three Cheers for Catherine the Great!* by Cari Best/ Giselle Potter (Russian Borscht ~ Beet and Vegetable Soup Recipe)

☐ _____

☐ _____

☐ _____

February ~ Pancakes

☐ *Potato Pancakes All Around* by Marilyn Hirsh (Hanukkah ~ Potato Pancake Recipe)

☐ *Carlos and the Cornfields* by Jan Romero Stevens/ Jeanne Arnold (Blue Corn Pancakes Recipe)

☐ *Hey, Pancakes!* by Tamson Weston/ Stephen Gammell (Grandma's Pancakes Recipe)

☐ *Pancakes, Pancakes!* by Eric Carle (Pancake Recipe)

☐ *Fannie in the Kitchen* by Deborah Hopkinson/ Nancy Carpenter (Fannie Farmer's Famous Griddle Cakes Recipe)

☐ *Talluah in the Kitchen* by Nancy Wolff (Amazing Blueberryalicious Pancakes Recipe)

☐ *Miss Mable's Table* by Deborah Chandra/ Max Grover (Pancake Recipe)

☐ *A Mountain of Blintzes* by Barbara Diamond Goldin/ Anik McGrory (Blintz ~ Crepe/Thin-Filled Pancake Recipe)

☐ *Pancakes for Supper* by Anne Isaacs/ Mark Teague (Pancake Recipe)

☐ *When Johnny Comes Marching Home* by P. Gilmore/ Todd Ouren---Provides a complete version of the song as well as its historical context and significance (Johnnycakes Recipe)

☐ *Mama Panya's Pancakes: A Village Tale from Kenya* by Mary and Rich Chamberlin/ Julia Cairns (Mama Panya's Pancake Recipe)

☐ *Uncle Phil's Diner* by Helena Clare Pittman (Uncle Phil's Blueberry Pancake Recipe)

☐ _____

☐ _____

☐ _____

March ~ Breads

☐ *Purim Play* by Roni Schotter/ Marylin Hafner (Purim Cookies ~ Apricot-Orange Hamantaschen Recipe)

☐ *Cakes and Miracles* by Barbara Diamond Goldin/ Erika Weihs (Purim ~ Hamantashen: A Traditional Purim Pastry Recipe)

☐ *Pretzels by the Dozen* by Angela Elwell Hunt/ Bill Dodge (Pretzel Recipe)

☐ *Gladys Goes Out to Lunch* by Derek Anderson (Banana Bread Recipe)

☐ *Sun Bread* by Elisa Kleven (Sun Bread Recipe)

☐ *Aunt Pitty Patty's Piggy* by Jim Aylesworth/ Barbara McClintock (Cornbread Recipe)

☐ *The Little Red Hen and the Ear of Wheat* by Mary Finch/ Elizabeth Bell (Whole Wheat Bread Recipe)

☐ *Watch Out for the Chicken Feet in Your Soup* by Tomie de Paola (Bread Dolls Recipe)

☐ *Auntie Anne, My Story* by Anne Beiler/ Freimen Stoltzfus (Pretzel Story)

☐ *Old Thunder and Miss Raney* by Sharon Darrow/ Kathryn Brown (Biscuit Recipe)

☐ *George and Diggety* by Maggie Stern/ Blanche Sims (Delicious Dog Biscuit Recipe)

☐ *The Story of Easter* by Aileen Fisher/ Stefano Vitale (Hot Crossed Buns Recipe)

☐ *Everybody Bakes Bread* by Norah Dooley/ Peter J. Thornton (Cultural Bread Recipes)

☐ *Viking Longship* by Mick Manning/ Brita Granstrom (Birka Bread Recipe)

☐ _____

☐ _____

☐ _____

April ~ Sweets to the Sweet

☐ *Pie in the Sky* by Lois Ehlert (Very Cherry-Filled Pie Recipe)

☐ *Cook-A-Doodle-Doo* by Janet Stevens/ Susan Stevens Crummel (Teamwork ~ Great-Granny's Magnificent Strawberry Shortcake Recipe)

☐ *Cranberry Easter* by Wende and Harry Devlin (Cranberry Cobbler Recipe)

☐ *A Drop of Honey* by Djemma Bider/ Armen Kojoyian (Baklava Recipe)

☐ *How Nanita Learned to Make Flan* by Campbell Geeslin/ Petra Mathers (Mexican Culture ~ Flan Recipe)

☐ *Don't Go!* by Jane Breskin Zelben (Pumpkin Vanilla Chip Cookie Recipe)

☐ *The Moon Might be Milk* by Lisa Shulman/ Will Hillenbrand (Gran's Sugar Cookie Moons)

☐ *A Cow, A Bee, A Cookie, and Me* by Meredith Hooper/ Alison Bartlett (Honey Cookie Recipe)

☐ *Pearl's Passover: A Family Celebration* by Jane Breskin Zalben (Cranberry Mandelbrot, Apple-and-Walnut Haroset, Date-and-Almond Haroset Recipes)

☐ *The Bye-Bye Pie* by Sharon Jennings/ Ruth Ohi (Family Traditions ~ Pecan Pie with Chocolate Sauce Recipe)

☐ *Valerie and the Silver Pear* by Benjamin Darling/ Daniel Lane (Pear Pie Recipe)

☐ *Honey Cookies* by Meredith Hooper/ Alison Bartl (Honey Biscuit Recipe)

☐ *Mr. Cookie Baker* by Monica Wellington (Recipes for Sugar Cookies, Chocolate Chip Cookies, Peanut Butter Cookies, Oatmeal Cookies)

☐ *Road-Maker's Munch* by Josephine Croser (Good read with *Mike Mulligan,* Recipe included)

☐ *Little Red Riding Hood: A Newfangled Prairie Tale* by Lisa Campbell Ernst (Wheat Berry Muffins Recipe)

☐ *Goldilocks and the Three Bears* by Jim Aylesworth/ Barbara McClintock (Mama Bear's Porridge Cookies ~ Oatmeal Cookie Recipe)

☐ *Mud Pie Annie* by Sue Buchanan and Dana Shafer/ Joy Allen (Dirt Cake, No Bake Fudge Cookies, Mississippi Mud Cake, Sand Tart Recipes)

☐ *Warthogs in the Kitchen* by Pamela Duncan Edwards/ Henry Cole (Cupcake Recipe)

☐ *Sunday Potatoes, Monday Potatoes* by Vicky Shiefman/ Louise August (Potato Pudding Recipe)

☐ *Boom Town* by Sonia Levitin/ Cat Bowman Smith (Gooseberry Pie Recipe)

☐ *Selina and the Shoo-Fly Pie* by Barbara Smucker/ Janet Wilson (Shoe Fly Pie with a Wet Bottom Recipe)

☐ **Sofie's Role** by Amy Heath/ Sheila Hamanaka (Marzipan ~ Cinnamon Star Cookies Recipe)

☐ _____

☐ _____

☐ _____

May ~ Cakes

☐ **Whopper Cake** by Karma Wilson/ Will Hillenbrand (Whopper Chocolate Cake Recipe)

☐ **A Cake All for Me** by Karen Magnuson Beil/ Paul Meisel (Sharing ~ Polka-Dot Cake)

☐ **Seven Silly Eaters** by Mary Ann Hoberman/ Marla Frazee (Pink Lemonade Cake Recipe found at http://www.maryannhoberman.com/cake.html)

☐ **Warthogs in the Kitchen** by Pamela Duncan Edwards/ Henry Cole (Cupcake Recipes)

☐ **Valentine Foxes** by Clyde Watson/ Wendy Watson (Pound Cake Recipe)

☐ **Cranberry Valentine** by Wende and Harry Devlin (Cranberry Upside-Down Cake)

☐ **Amelia and Eleanor Go for a Ride** by Pam Munoz Ryan/ Brian Selznick (Angel Food Cake with Whipped Cream and Strawberries Recipe)

☐ **Don't Forget** by Patricia Lakin/ Ted Rand (Orange Sponge Cake Recipe)

☐ **Miss Poppy and the Honey Cake** by Elizabeth MacDonald/ Claire Smith (Honey Cake Recipe)

☐ **Auntee Edna** by Ethel Footman Smothers/ Wil Clay (Tea Cakes Recipe)

☐ **Goody O'Grumpity** by Carol Ryrie Brink/ Ashley Wolff (Autumn ~ Spice Cake)

☐ **Thunder Cake** by Patricia Polacco (Rainy Days ~ My Grandma's Thunder Cake)

☐ ***Eight Animals Bake a Cake*** by Susan Middletown Elya/ Lee Chapman (Pineapple Upside Down Cake Recipe)

☐ ***Saturdays and Tea Cakes*** by Lester Laminack/ Chris Soentpiet (Mammaw's Special Teacakes Recipe)

☐ ***My Pop Pop and Me*** by Irene Smalls/ Cathy Ann Johnson (Lemon Bar Cake Bake)

☐ ***Bruno the Baker*** by Lars Klinting (Birthday ~ Cake Recipe)

☐ ***Baby Babka, The Gorgeous Genius*** by Jane Breskin Zalben (Chocolate Babka ~ Chocolate Cake Loaf Recipe)

☐ ***Beverly Billingsly Takes the Cake*** by Alexander Stadler (Simple Cake Recipe)

☐ ***Don't Forget*** by Patricia Lakin/ Ted Rand (Tribute to Holocaust Survivors ~ Orange Sponge Cake Recipe)

☐ ***Marcellus' Birthday Cake*** by Lorraine Simeon/ Petra Rohr-Rouendaal (Cake with a Chocolate Covering Recipe)

☐ ***A Birthday Cake for Little Bear*** by Max Velthuijs (Little Bear's Chocolate Birthday Cake Recipe)

☐ _____

☐ _____

☐ _____

ഀഀഀഀ ൟൟൟൟ

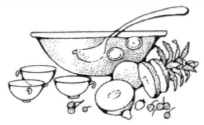

June ~ Thirst Quenchers and Summer Snacks

☐ *Cranberry Summer* by Wende and Harry Devlin (Cranberry Punch Recipe)

☐ *Lulu's Lemonade* by Barbara deRubertis/ Paige Billin-Frye (Lemonade Recipe)

☐ *The Greatest Potatoes* by Penelope Stowell/ Sharon Watts (Potato Chip Recipe)

☐ *The Lemon Sisters* by Andrea Cheng/ Tatjana Mai-Wyss (Lemon Ice Recipe)

☐ *Nana's Rice Pie* by Laurie Lazzaro Knowlton/ Joyce Haynes (Sweet Rice Pie Recipe)

☐ *Benito's Sopaipillas* by Ana Baca/ Anthony Accardo (Sopaipillas Recipe)

☐ *The Moon Might be Milk* by Lisa Shulman/ Will Hillenbrand (Gran's Sugar Cookie Moon Recipe)

☐ *Arianna and the Strawberry Tea* by Maria Fasal Faulconer/ Katy Keck Arnzteen (Strawberry Tea and Chocolate Tarts)

☐ *Bananas* by Jacqueline Farmer/ Page Eastburn O'Rourke (Simple Banana Recipe includes making the perfect summertime treat: Banana Splits)

☐ *No More Cookies!* by Paeony Lewis/ Brita Granstrom (Magic Monkey Bananas ~ Chocolate-Covered Bananas Recipe)

☐ _____

☐ _____

July ~ Variety

☐ ***'T Pousette et'T Poulette : A Cajun Hansel and Gretel***
by Sheila Hebert Collins/ Patrick Soper (La Sauce Patate
Recipe)

☐ ***Les Trois Cochons*** by Sheila Hebert Collins/ Patrick
Soper (Grillades-Meat and Grits Recipe)

☐ ***Cendrillon: A Cajun Cinderella*** by Sheila Hebert
Collins/ Patrick Soper (Red Beans and Rice Recipe)

☐ ***What Zeesie Saw on Delancey Street*** by Elsa Okon Rael/
Marjorie Priceman (Two Tradional Jewish Recipes)

☐ ***When Zaydeh Danced on Eldridge Street*** by Elsa Okon
Rael/ Marjorie Priceman (Two Traditional Jewish Recipes)

☐ ***Pigs in the Pantry*** by Amy Axelrod/ Sharon McGinley-
Nally (Sickness ~ Chili Recipe)

☐ ***On Top of Spaghetti*** by Paul Brett Johnson (Spaghetti
and Meatball Recipe)

☐ ***Noodle Man: The Pasta Superhero*** by April Pulley
Sayre/ Stephen Costanza (Perfect Pasta Recipe)

☐ ***Three Days on a River in a Red Canoe*** by Vera B.
Williams (Dumplings and Fruit Stew Recipes)

☐ ***The Greatest Potatoes*** by Penelope Stowell/ Sharon
Watts (Potato Chip Recipe)

☐ ***Everybody Brings Noodles*** by Norah Dooley/ Peter J.
Thornton (Cultural Noodle/Pasta Recipes)

☐ _____

☐ _____

August ~ Cultural Foods

☐ *Pizza at Sally's* by Monica Wellington (Pizza Recipe)
☐ *Pizza for the Queen* by Nancy F. Castaldo/ Melisande Potter (Pizza Margherita Recipe)
☐ *The Pizza That We Made* by Joan Holub/ Lynne Cravath (Pizza Recipe)
☐ *Crepes by Suzette* by Monica Wellington (Crepe Recipe)
☐ *Domitila: a Cinderella Tale from the Mexican Tradition* by Jewell Reinhart Coburn/ Connie McLennan (Domitila's Nopales Recipe)
☐ *Jalapeno Bagels* by Natasha Wing/ Robert Casilla (International Day ~ Complete with Jewish and Mexican Recipes)
☐ *Jacques et la Canne A Sucre: A Cajun Jack and the Beanstalk* by Sheila Hebert Collins/ Alison Davis Lyne (Shrimp or Crawfish Etoufee Recipe)
☐ *Chicks and Salsa* by Aaron Reynolds/ Paulette Bogan (Cinco De Mayo ~ Hog Wild Nachos, Quackamole, and Rooster's Roasted Salsa Recipes)
☐ *Blanchette et les Sept Petits Cajuns: A Cajun Snow White* by Sheila Hebert-Collins/ Patrick Soper (Blanchette's Chicken and Sausage Jambalaya)
☐ *The Runaway Rice Cake* by Ying Chang Compestine/ Tungwai Chau (Chinese New Year ~ *Nian Gao* or Good Luck Cake Recipe)
☐ *Carlos and the Squash Plant* by Jan Romero Stevens/ Jeanne Arnold (Growing Gardens ~ Calabacitas Recipe)

☐ *The Story of Noodles* by Ying Chang Compestine/ Yongsheng Xuan (Long-Life Noodle and Sauce Recipe)

☐ *Saturday Sancocho* by Leyla Torres (Shopping ~ Mama Ana's Chicken Sancocho Recipe)

☐ *Kallaloo!: A Caribbean Tale* by David and Phillis Gershator/ Diane Greenseid (Kallaloo Soup Recipe)

☐ *How My Family Lives in America* by Susan Kuklin (Various Recipes)

☐ *I Lost My Tooth in Africa* by Penda Diakite/ Baba Waque Diakite (African Onion Soup Recipe)

☐ *Chiles for Benito* by Ana Baca/ Anthony Accardo (Red Chile Sauce Recipe)

☐ *Everybody Cooks Rice* by Norah Dooley/ Peter J. Thornton (Cultural Rice Recipes)

☐ *This Is the Way We Eat Our Lunch: A Book About Children around the World* by Edith Baer/ Steve Bjorkman (Fruit Salad, Hummus, Wild Rice Soup Recipes)

☐ *Market Days: From Market to Market around the World* by Madhur Jaffrey/ Marti Shohet (Large Variety of Cultural Food Recipes)

☐ *Bee-bim Bop!* by Linda Sue Park/ Ho Baek Lee (Korean Mix-Mix Rice Recipe)

☐ *The Tortilla Quilt* by Jane Tenorio-Coscarelli (Homemade Tortilla Recipe)

☐ *The Tamale Quilt* by Jane Tenorio-Coscarelli (Homemade Tamale Recipe)

☐ _____

☐ _____

(See other Cultural books by Norah Dooley and Peter J. Thornton listed under January Soup, March Bread, and July Variety)

171

September ~ Apple Harvest

☐ *A Song for Lena* by Hilary Horder Hippely/ Leslie Baker (Harvest Time ~ Grandma's Apple Strudel Recipe)

☐ *Apple Farmer Annie* by Monica Wellington (Recipes for Applesauce, Muffins, and Cake)

☐ *Country Bear's Good Neighbor* by Larry Dane Brimner/ Ruth Tietjen Councell (Country Bear's Good Neighbor Apple Cake Recipe)

☐ *The Apple Pie Tree* by Zoe Hall/ Shari Halpern (Apple Pie Recipe)

☐ *How to Make an Apple Pie and See the World* by Marjorie Priceman (Apple Pie Recipe)

☐ *Apple Cake* by Nienke van Hichtum/ Marjan van Zeyl (Apple Cake Recipe)

☐ *Apple Batter* by Deborah Turney Zagwyn (Apple Crumble Recipe)

☐ *Cranberry Mystery* by Wende and Harry Devlin (Grandmother's Famous Cranberry Pie-Pudding Recipe)

☐ *Remember, Grandma?* by Laura Langston/ Lindsey Gardiner (Grandma's Mile-High Apple Pie Recipe)

☐ *Happy New Year, Beni* by Jane Breskin Zalben (Rosh Hashanah ~ Raisin Challah Recipe)

☐ *Apples, Apples, Apples* by Nancy Elizabeth Wallace (Applesauce Recipe)

☐ *Apples* by Jacqueline Farmer/ Phyllis Limbacher Tildes (Awesome Apple Pie Recipe)

☐ _____

☐ _____

October ~ Autumn Treasures and Pumpkins

☐ *Cranberry Autumn* by Wende and Harry Devlin (Cranberry Squares Recipe)

☐ *Pumpkin Fiesta* by Caryn Yacowitz/ Joe Cepeda (Pumpkin Soup Recipe)

☐ *The Bake-Shop Ghost* by Jacqueline K. Ogburn/ Marjorie Priceman (Ghost-Pleasing Chocolate Cake Recipe)

☐ *Cranberry Halloween* by Wende and Harry Devlin (Cranberry Dessert Recipe)

☐ *Halloween Pie* by Michael O. Tunnell/ Kevin O'Malley (Halloween Pumpkin Pie Recipe)

☐ *Pumpkin Day!* by Nancy Elizabeth Wallace (Toasted Pumpkin Seeds, Pumpkin Muffins, Pumpkin Pancakes Recipes)

☐ *Pumpkins* by Jacqueline Farmer/ Phyllis Limbacher Tildes (Pumpkin Maple Pie and Seed Roasting Recipes)

☐ *Turtle and Snake's Spooky Halloween* by Kate Spohn (Spooky Pond Punch)

☐ *Maria Molina and the Days of the Dead* by Kathleen Krull/ Enrique O. Sanchez (Traditional Bread of the Dead)

173

□ _____
□ _____

November ~ Thanksgiving Time

□ *Cranberry Thanksgiving* by Wende and Harry Devlin (Grandmother's Famous Cranberry Bread Recipe)
□ *Albert's Thanksgiving* by Leslie Tryon (Thanksgiving Feast ~ Scrumptious Pumpkin Pizza Pie Recipe)
□ *The Giant Carrot* by Jan Peck/ Barry Root (Little Isabelle's Carrot Puddin' Recipe)
□ *Two Old Potatoes and Me* by John Coy/ Carolyn Fisher (Mashed Potato Recipe)
□ *The Popcorn Book* by Tomie de Paola (Popcorn Recipes)
□ _____
□ _____
□ _____

December ~ Holiday Yummies and Christmas Cookies

☐ *Tony's Bread* by Tomie dePaola (Christmas bread ~ Panettone Recipe)

☐ *Happy Winter* by Karen Gundersheimer (Fudge Cake Recipe)

☐ *Hot Fudge* by James Howe/ Jeff Mack (Mr. Monroe's Famous Fudge Recipe)

☐ *Too Many Tamales* by Gary Soto/ Ed Martinez (Christmas ~ Tamales Recipe)

☐ *The Runaway Latkes* by Leslie Kimmelman/ Paul Yalowitz (Hanukkah ~ Latkes Recipe)

☐ *Grandma's Latkes* by Malka Drucker/ Eve Chwast (Hanukkah ~ Latkes Recipe)

☐ *Latkes and Applesauce* by Fran Manushkin/ Robin Spowart (Hanukkah ~ Elaborate Latkes Recipe)

☐ *Inside-Out Grandma: A Hanukkah Story* by Joan Rothenberg (Hanukkah ~ Potato Latke Recipe)

☐ *Latkes, Latkes Good to Eat: A Chanukah Story* by Naomi Howland (Chanukah—also known as Hanukkah—Latkes Recipe)

☐ *Cranberry Christmas* by Wende and Harry Devlin (Maggie's Favorite Cranberry Cookies Recipe)

☐ *Snowballs* by Lois Ehlert (Popcorn Ball Recipe)

☐ *Jingle the Christmas Clown* by Tomie dePaola (Stelline d'Oro or Star Cookies Recipe)

☐ *Mother Grumpy's Dog Biscuits: A True Tail* by Becky Wilson-Kelly (Mother Grumpy's Chocolate Chip Bumpy Cookies Recipe)

☐ *No More Chocolate Chips* by Linda Michellebaron (Chocolate Chip Cookies Recipe)

☐ *The Gingerbread Man* by Jim Aylesworth/ Barbara McClintock (Make Your Own Gingerbread Man ~ Gingerbread Cookie Recipe)

☐ *Mr. Cookie Baker* by Monica Wellington (Cookie Recipe)

☐ *The Christmas Cookie Tree* by Ruth Hershey Irion (Gingerbread Cookie Recipes)

☐ *Christmas Turtles* by Sara Ann Denson/ Tara McMillen (Christmas Turtle Candy Recipe)

☐ _____

☐ _____

☐ _____

Plum & Berry Pleasures
(including other berry books that don't have recipes but tempt the palate during berry picking season May-June)

☐ *Making Plum Jam* by John Warren Stewig/ Kevin O'Malley (Plum Jam Recipe)

☐ *Purple Delicious Blackberry Jam* by Lisa Westberg Peters/ McGregor
☐ *Blueberries for Sal* by Robert McCloskey
☐ *Jamberry* by Bruce Degen
☐ *When the Rain Stops* by Sheila Cole/ Henri Sorensen
☐ *Blueberries for the Queen* by Katherine Paterson/ Susan Jeffers
☐ *Mother Raspberry* by Maurice Careme/ Marie Wabbes
☐ *Dr. Welch and the Great Grape Story* by Mary Lou Carney/ Sherry Meidell
☐ *Blackberry Booties* by Tricia Gardella/ Glo Coalson
☐ *Blueberry Shoe* by Ann Dixon/ Evon Zerbetz
☐ *Molly and the Strawberry Day* by Pam Conrad/ Mary Szilagyi
☐ *Jam and Jelly by Holly and Nellie* by Gloria Whelan/ Gijsbert Van Frankenhuyzen
☐ *The First Strawberries* by Joseph Bruchac/ Anna Vojtech
☐ *The Giant Jam Sandwich* by John Vernon Lord/ Janet Burroway
☐ _____
☐ _____
☐ _____

Special thank you to Shalome Westberg for helping extensively with the development of this feast.

A Picture-Perfect Photo Album for Families

I have spoken to many parents who bemoan the fact that their child will not read and does like to read. Books have long been stereotyped as "schoolwork", thus children often shun them. Within the pages of this book, I have attempted to suggest how to include books into real life happenings. Books can still be a large part of life learning if we plant the habit early and pleasantly. I would like to see books presented not as something a child *has to do* but as something he *wants to do*.

Is your family going to the beach? Having a family reunion? Researching your family roots? Handling the death of a grandparent? Planning a vacation? Picture books can get your child reading while getting you through the planning and the adventure.

Is your child studying the Civil War? Mapping out the Underground Railroad? Wanting to explore the world? Doing a history project on famous people? Picture books add a sprinkle of educational exposure as well and make learning inviting even to reluctant, frustrated, and slow readers.

Remember, illustrated books are the photo albums that teach your child to learn to care about the world and people around them. It is up to you to tell him the story.

Adoption

☐ *Jin Woo* by Eve Bunting/ Chris K. Soentpiet

☐ *Over the Moon* by Karen Katz

☐ *Allison* by Allen Say

☐ *Everytime You Call Me Mommy: An Adoption Blessing* by Kimberly Kane/ Bitsey Crismon

☐ *I Don't Have Your Eyes* by Carrie A. Kitze/ Rob Williams

☐ *The Red Blanket* by Eliza Thomas/ Joe Cepeda

☐ *The Red Thread* by Grace Lin

☐ *Tell me Again about the Night I was Born* by Jamie Lee Curtis/ Laura Cornell

☐ *The Day We Met You* by Phoebe Koehler

☐ *Adoption is for Always* by Linda Walvoord Girard/ Judith Friedman

☐ *I Love You like Crazy Cakes* by Rose Lewis/ Jane Dyer

☐ *When I Met You* by Adrienne Ehlert Bashista/ Christine Sykes

☐ *Families are Forever* by Craig Shemin/ John McCoy

☐ *Through Moon and Stars and Night Skies* by Ann Turner/ James Graham Hale

☐ *Happy Adoption Day* by John McCutcheon/ Julie Paschkis

☐ *Every Year on Your Birthday* by Rose A. Lewis/ Jane Dyer

☐ *A Quilt of Wishes* by Teresa Orem Werner/ Nathan Tremlin

☐ *Three Names of Me* by Mary Cummings/ Lin Wang

☐ *Finding Joy* by Marion Coste/ Yong Chen

☐ *Bringing Asha Home* by Uma Krishnaswami/ Jamel Akib

☐ *The White Swan Express* by Jean Davies Okimoto/ Elaine M. Aoki/ Meilo So

☐ *The Mulberry Bird* by Anne Braff Brodzinsky/ Diana L. Stanley

☐ *My Mei Mei* by Ed Young

☐ *The Coffee Can Kid* by Jan Czech/ Maurie J. Manning

☐ *Lucy's Family Tree* by Karen Halvorsen Schreck/ Stephen Gassler III

☐ *We Wanted You* by Liz Rosenberg/ Peter Catalanotto

☐ *Did My First Mother Love Me?* by Kathryn Ann Miller/ Jami Moffett

☐ _____

180

☐ _____

Angels

☐ *Angels, Angels Everywhere* by Tomie dePaola

☐ *My Guardian Dear* by Susan A. Brindle/ Miriam A. Lademan

☐ *Pascual and the Kitchen Angels* by Tomie dePaola

☐ *Country Angel Christmas* by Tomie dePaola

☐ *God Bless the Gargoyles* by Dav Pilkey

☐ *The Acrobat and the Angel* by Mark Shannon/ David Shannon

☐ *Angel in the Waters* by Regina Doman/ Ben Hatke

☐ *The Angels' Alphabet* by Hilda Van Stockum

☐ *Angels Among Us* by Leena Lane/ Elena Baboni

☐ *Angels Watching Over Me* by Julia Durango/ Elisa Kleven

☐ *The Littlest Angel* by Charles Tazewell/ Paul Micich

☐ *Angel of God, What's Your Name?* by Rebecca McNall/ Joan Hutson

☐ _____

☐ _____

෯෯෯෯   ෨෨෨෨

Apples and Oranges...and Pumpkin Harvest

☐ *The Apple Doll* by Elisa Kleven

☐ *Apples* by Gail Gibbons

☐ *Autumn is for Apples* by Michelle Knudsen/ Denise Fernando

☐ *The Seasons of Arnold's Apple Tree* by Gail Gibbons

☐ *Apples and Pumpkins* by Anne Rockwell/ Lizzy Rockwell

☐ *How to Make an Apple Pie and See the World* by Marjorie Priceman

☐ *Ten Apples Up on Top* by Dr. Seuss/ Roy McKie

☐ *Ten Red Apples* by Pat Hutchins

☐ *Apple Picking Time* by Michele B. Slawson/ Deborah Kogan Ray

☐ *The Apple Pie that Papa Baked* by Lauren Thompson/ Jonathan Bean

☐ *Apple Fractions* by Jerry Pallotta/ Rob Bolster

☐ *Apple Farmer Annie* by Monica Wellington

☐ *Applesauce* by Shirley Kurtz

☐ *Apples to Oregon* by Deborah Hopkinson/ Nancy Carpenter

☐ *Our Apple Tree* by Gorel Kristina Naslund/ Kristina Digman

☐ *How do Apples Grow* by Betsy Maestro

☐ *The Apple Cake* by Nienke Van Hichtum

☐ *Apple Cider-Making Days* by Ann Purmell/ Joanne Friar

☐ *A Gift of Gracias* by Julia Alvarez/ Beatriz Vidal

☐ *Armadillo's Orange* by Jim Arnosky

☐ *Oranges on Golden Mountain* by Elizabeth Partridge/ Aki Sogabe

☐ *The Three Golden Oranges* by Alma Flor Ada/ Reg Cartwright

☐ *An Orange for Frankie* by Patricia Polacco

☐ *Christmas Oranges* by Linda Bethers/ Ben Sowards

☐ *The Love for Three Oranges* by Sergei Prokofiev/ Elzbieta Gaudasinska

☐ *The Big Pumpkin* by Erica Silverman/ S.D. Schindler

☐ *Pumpkin Soup* by Helen Cooper

☐ *Pumpkin Circle* by George Levenson/ Shmuel Thaler

☐ *Pumpkins, Pumpkins* by Jeanne Titherington

☐ *The Pumpkin Patch Parable* by Liz Curtis Higgs

☐ *The Pumpkin Blanket* by Deborah Turney Zagwyn

☐ *From Seed to Pumpkin* by Wendy Pfeffer/ James Graham Hale

☐ *Pumpkins: A Story for a Field* by Mary Lyn Ray/ Barry Root

☐ *The Pumpkin Fair* by Eve Bunting/ Eileen Christelow

☐ *Pumpkin Hill* by Elizabeth Spurr/ Whitney Martin

☐ *Patty's Pumpkin Patch* by Teri Sloat

☐ *When the Frost is on the Punkin'* by James Whitcomb Riley/ Glenna Lang

☐ *Pumpkin Fiesta* by Caryn Yacowitz/ Joe Cepeda

☐ *The Pumpkin Runner* by Marsha Diane Arnold/ Brad Sneed

☐ *The Great Pumpkin Switch* by Megan McDonald/ Ted Lewin

☐ *The Pumpkin Book* by Gail Gibbons

☐ *Too Many Pumpkins* by Linda White/ Megan Lloyd

☐ *Pumpkin Moonshine* by Tasha Tudor

☐ *How Many Seeds in a Pumpkin?* by Margaret McNamara/ G. Brian Karas

☐ *The Biggest Pumpkin Ever* by Steven Kroll/ Jeni Bassett

☐ *Corgiville Fair* by Tasha Tudor

☐ *Christopher's Harvest Time* by Elsa Maartman Beskow

☐ *Hello, Harvest Moon* by Ralph Fletcher/ Kate Kiesler

☐ *I Know it's Autumn* by Eileen Spinelli/ Nancy Hayashi

☐ *Itse Selu: Cherokee Harvest Festival* by Daniel Pennington/ Don Stewart

☐ *Harvest* by Waldherr Kris

☐ *Harvest Home* by Jane Yolen/ Greg Shed

☐ *Autumn Equinox: Celebrating the Harvest* by Ellen Jackson/ Jan Davey Ellis

☐ _____

☐ _____

Arctic

☐ *The Blizzard's Robe* by Robert Sabuda

☐ *Kumak's Fish* by Michael Bania

☐ *Little Cliff and the Cold Place* by Clifton L. Taulbert/ E.B. Lewis

☐ *Very First Last Time* by Jan Andrews/ Ian Wallace

☐ *Tundra Mouse Mountain* by Riitta Jalonen/ Kristiina Louhi

☐ *Arctic Tundra* by Donald M. Silver/ Patricia Wynne

☐ *Arctic Lights, Arctic Nights* by Debbie Miller/ Jon Van Zyle

☐ *The Polar Bear Son* by Lydia Dabcovich

☐ *Tupag the Dreamer* by Kerry Hannula Brown/ Linda Saport

☐ *This Place is Cold* by Vicki Cobb/ Barbara LaVallee

☐ *Snow Bear* by Jean Craighead George/ Wendell Minor

☐ *A Polar Bear Journey* by Debbie Miller/ Jon Van Zyle

☐ *Welcome to the Ice House* by Jane Yolen/ Laura Regan

☐ _____

☐ _____

Take Me Out to the Ballgame

☐ *Louis Sockalexis: Native American Baseball Pioneer* by Bill Wise/ Bill Farnsworth

☐ *My Baseball Book* by Gail Gibbons

☐ *Baseball Hour* by Carol Nevius/ Bill Thomson

☐ *Take Me out to the Ballgame* by jack Norworth/ Alec Gillman

☐ *How Georgie Radbourne Saved Baseball* by David Shannon

☐ *Zachary's Ball* by Matt Tavares

☐ *Mudball* by Matt Tavares

☐ *The Shot Heard Round the World* by Phil Bildner/ C.F. Payne

☐ *86 Years: the Legend of the Boston Red Sox* by Melinda Boroson

☐ *Nick Plays Baseball* by Rachel Isadora

☐ *Home Run: Story of Babe Ruth* by Robert Burleigh/ Mike Wimmer

☐ *H is for Home Run: A Baseball Alphabet* by Brad Herzog/ Melanie Rose-Popp

☐ *The Legend of the Curse of the Bambino* by Dan Shaughnessy/ C.F. Payne

☐ *The Babe and I* by David Adler/ Terry Widener

☐ *Team Mates* by Peter Golenbock/ Paul Bacon

☐ *Lou Gehrig: The Luckiest Man* by David Adler/ Terry Widener

☐ *Baseball Saved Us* by Ken Mochizuki/ Dom Lee

☐ *Satchel Paige* by Lesa Cline-Ransome/ James Ransome

☐ *Coming Home: A True Story about Josh Gibson* by Nanette Mellage/ Cornelius Van Wright and Ying-Hwa Hu

☐ *Cal Ripken, Jr.: The Longest Season* by Ron Mazellan

☐ *Casey at the Bat: A Ballad* by Ernest Lawrence Thayer/ Christopher Bing/ Patricia Polacco (many other illustrated versions available)

☐ *Hank Aaron: Brave in Every Way* by Peter Golenbock/ Paul Lee

☐ *Play Ball!* by Jorge Posada/ Robert Burleigh/ Raul Colon

☐ *Out of the Ballpark* by Alex Rodriquez/ Frank Morrison

☐ *Let Them Play* by Margot Theis Raven/ Chris Ellison

☐ *Roberto Clemente: Pride of the Pittsburgh Pirates* by Jonah Winter/ Raul Colon

☐ *Shoeless Joe and Black Betsy* by Phil Bildner/ C.F. Payne

☐ _____

☐ _____

(For Girls)
☐ *Girl Wonder: A Baseball Story in Nine Innings* by Deborah Hopkinson/ Terry Widener

☐ *Players in Pigtails* by Shana Corey/ Rebecca Gibbon

☐ *Mama Played Baseball* by David Adler/ Chris O'Leary

☐ *Just Like Josh Gibson* by Angela Johnson/ Beth Peck

☐ *Dirt on their Skirts* by Doreen Rappaport/ Lyndall Callan/ E.B. Lewis

☐ *Mighty Jackie: The Strike-Out Queen* by Marissa Moss/ C.F. Payne

☐ _____

☐ _____

Black History Month

☐ *Papa's Mark* by Gwendolyn Battle-Lavert/ Colin Bootman

☐ *Freedom School, Yes!* by Amy Littlesugar/ Floyd Cooper

☐ *Drylongso* by Virginia Hamilton/ Jerry Pinkney

☐ *Goin' Somplace Special* by Patricia C. McKissack/ Jerry Pinkney

☐ *Mirandy and Brother Wind* by Patricia C. McKissack/ Jerry Pinkney

☐ *Sam and the Tigers* by Julius Lester/ Jerry Pinkney

☐ *From Miss Ida's Porch* by Sandra Belton/ Floyd Cooper

☐ *The Hired-Man ~ A Folktale* by Robert D. San Souci/ Jerry Pinkney

☐ *Show Way* by Jacqueline Woodson/ Hudson Talbott

☐ *The Sunday Outing* by Gloria Jean Pinkney/ Jerry Pinkney

☐ *Back Home* by Gloria Jean Pinkney/ Jerry Pinkney

☐ *I Want to Be* by Thylias Moss/ Jerry Pinkney

☐ *John Henry* by Julius Lester/ Jerry Pinkney

☐ *Jim Limber Davis: A Black Orphan in the Confederate White House* by Rickey Pittman/ Judith Hierstein

☐ *Rosa* by Nikki Giovanni/ Bryan Collier

☐ *Sister Anne's Hands* by Marybeth Lorbiecki/ Wendy Popp

☐ *Grandmama's Pride* by Becky Birtha/ Colin Bootman

- ☐ *White Socks Only* by Evelyn Coleman/ Tyrone Geter
- ☐ *Freedom on the Menu* by Carole Boston Weatherford/ Jerome LaGarrique
- ☐ *The School is not White* by Doreen Rappaport/ Curtis James
- ☐ *A Sweet Smell of Roses* by Angela Johnson/ Eric Velasquez
- ☐ *The Story of Ruby Bridges* by Robert Coles/ George Ford
- ☐ *The Talking Eggs ~ A Folktale* by Robert D. San Souci/ Jerry Pinkney
- ☐ *The Secret of the Stones* by Robert D. San Souci/ Jerry Pinkney
- ☐ *Black Cowboy, Wild Horses* by Julius Lester/ Jerry Pinkney
- ☐ *Mississippi Morning* by Ruth Vander Zee/ Floyd Cooper
- ☐ *Oh Lord, I Wish I was a Buzzard* by Polly Greenberg/ Aliki
- ☐ *Tar Beach* by Faith Ringgold
- ☐ *Working Cotton* by Sherley Anne Williams/ Carole Byard
- ☐ *Pink and Say* by Patricia Polacco
- ☐ *Who Owns the Sun* by Stacey Chbosky
- ☐ *Treemonisha* by Angela Shelf Medearis/ Michael Bryant
- ☐ *Chicken Sunday* by Patricia Polacco
- ☐ *Mr. Lincoln's Way* by Patricia Polacco

☐ *A Weed is a Flower ~ Life of George Washington Carver* by Aliki

☐ *Sweet, Sweet Memories* by Jacqueline Woodson/ Floyd Cooper

☐ *The Other Side* by Jacqueline Woodson/ E.B. Lewis

☐ *Coming On Home Soon* by Jacqueline Woodson/ E.B. Lewis

☐ *A Band of Angels* by Deborah Hopkinson/ Raul Colon

☐ *My Dream of Martin Luther King* by Faith Ringgold

☐ *Martin's Big Words* by Doreen Rappaport/ Bryan Collier

☐ *My Brother Martin: A Sister Remembers Growing Up with the Rev. Dr. Martin Luther King, Jr.* by Christine King Farris/ Chris Soentpiet

☐ *I Have a Dream* by Martin Luther King (Foreword by Coretta Scott King)

☐ *Circle Unbroken* by Margot Theis Raven/ E. B. Lewis

☐ *I've Seen the Promised Land* by Walter Dean Myers/ Leonard Jenkins

☐ *Ellington Was not a Street* by Ntozake Shange/ Kadir Nelson

☐ *Freedom Summer* by Deborah Wiles/ Jerome Laqarrique

☐ *Tanya's Reunion* by Valerie Flournoy/ Jerry Pinkney

☐ *God Bless the Child* by Billie Holiday, Jr., Arthur Herzog, Jerry Pinkney

☐ *Molly Bannaky* by Alice McGill/ Chris K. Soentpiet

☐ *Dear Benjamin Banneker* by Andrea David Pinkney/ Brian Pinkney

☐ *The Escape of Oney Judge: Martha Washington's Slave Finds Freedom* by Emily Arnold McCully

☐ _____

☐ _____

(*Any* books illustrated by Jerry Pinkney and *any* books written by Julius Lester are excellent books for this month.)

Careers & Economics

☐ *Building with Dad* by Carol Nevius/ Bill Thomson

☐ *What do Illustrators Do?* by Eileen Christelow

☐ *What do Authors Do?* by Eileen Christelow

☐ *If You Were a Writer* by Joan Lowery Nixon/ Bruce Degan

☐ *Little Nino's Pizzeria* by Karen Barbour

☐ *Career Day* by Anne F. Rockwell/ Lizzy Rockwell

☐ *The Fire* by Annette Griessman/ Leonid Gore

☐ *Policeman Lou and Policewoman Sue* by Lisa Desimini

☐ *Lions Aren't Scared of Shots: A Story for Children about Visiting the Doctor* by Howard J. Bennett/ M.S. Weber

☐ *Johnny on the Spot* by Edward Sorel

☐ *The Gardener* by Sarah Stewart/ David Small

☐ *The Money Tree* by Sarah Stewart/ David Small

☐ *Once Upon a Dime* by Nancy Kelly Allen/ Adam Doyle

☐ *Lemonade for Sale* by Stuart J. Murphy/ Tricia Tusa

☐ *The Penny Pot* by Stuart J. Murphy/ Lynne Woodcock Cravath

☐ *Jack of All Tails* by Kim E. Norman/ David H. Clark

☐ _____

☐ _____

China

☐ *Yeh-Shen* by Ai-Ling Louie/ Ed Young

☐ *Lon Po Po* by Ed Young

☐ *The Empty Pot* by Demi

☐ *One Grain of Rice* by Demi

☐ *Liang and the Magic Paintbrush* by Demi

☐ *The Greatest Power* by Demi

☐ *Daisy Comes Home* by Jan Brett

☐ *The Five Chinese Brothers* by Claire Huchet Bishop/ Kurt Wiese

☐ *Story about Ping* by Marjorie Flack/ Kurt Wiese

☐ *Tikki Tikki Tembo* by Arlene Mosel/ Blair Lent

☐ *The Seven Chinese Brothers* by Margaret Mahy/ Jean Tsang

☐ *Grandfather Counts* by Andrea Cheng/ Ange Zhang

☐ *Silent Lotus* by Jeanne M. Lee

☐ *In the Snow* by Huy Voun Lee

☐ *Kites: Magic Wishes that Fly up to the Sky* by Demi

☐ *Bitter Dumplings* by Jeanne M. Lee

☐ *The Magic Tapestry* by Demi

☐ *The Dragon's Tale and Other Animal Fables of the Chinese Zodiac* by Demi

☐ *The Greatest Treasure* by Demi

☐ *The Stonecutter* by Demi

☐ *The Artist and the Architect* by Demi

☐ *Under the Shade of the Mulberry Tree* by Demi

☐ *The Magic Boat* by Demi

☐ *Chen Ping and His Magic Axe* by Demi

☐ *The Seven Chinese Sisters* by Kathy Tucker/ Grace Lin

☐ *Goldfish and Chrysanthemums* by Andrea Cheng/ Michelle Chang

- ☐ *Chinatown* by William Low
- ☐ *The Weaving of a Dream* by Marilee Heyer
- ☐ *Happy, Happy Chinese New Year* by Demi
- ☐ *The Dancing Dragon* by Marcia Vaughan/ Stanley Wong Hoo Foon
- ☐ *Happy New Year! Kung-Hsi Fa-Ts'Ai* by Demi
- ☐ *Blue Willow* by Pam Conrad/ Susan Saelig Gallagher
- ☐ *The Willow Pattern Story* by Allan Drummond
- ☐ _____
- ☐ _____

Around the World and Beyond with Cinderella

- ☐ *Cinderella* by Marcia Brown
- ☐ *Cinderella* by K.Y. Craft
- ☐ *Cinderella* by Barbara McClintock
- ☐ *Fanny's Dream* by Caralyn Buehner/ Mark Buehner
- ☐ *The Golden Sandel: A **Middle Eastern** Cinderella Story* by Rebecca Hickox/ Will Hillenbrand
- ☐ *Adelita: A **Mexican** Cinderella Story* by Tomie dePaola

195

☐ *Little Gold Star: A **Spanish** American Cinderella Story* by Robert D. San Souci/ Sergio Martinez

☐ *Naya, the **Inuit** Cinderella* by Brittany Marceau-Chenkie/ Shelley Brookes

☐ *Smokey Mountain Rose: An **Appalachian** Cinderella* by Alan Schroeder/ Brad Sneed

☐ *Anklet for a Princess: A Cinderella Story from **India*** by Lila Mehta/Youshan Tang

☐ *The **Persian** Cinderella* by Shirley Climo/ Robert Florczak

☐ *The **Korean** Cinderella* by Shirley Climo/Ruth Heller

☐ *The Rough-Faced Girl: An **Algonquin Indian** Cinderella* by Rafe Martin/ David Shannon

☐ *Angkat: The **Cambodian** Cinderella* by Jewell Reinhart Coburn/ Edmund Flotte

☐ *Yeh-Shen: A Cinderella Story from **China*** by Ai-Ling Louie/ Ed Young

☐ *The **Egyptian** Cinderella* by Shirley Climo/ Ruth Heller

☐ *Sootface: An **Ojibwa** Cinderella Story* by Robert D. San Souci/ Daniel San Souci

☐ *Domitila: A Cinderella Tale from the **Mexican** Tradition* by Jewell Reinhart Coburn/ Connie McLennan

☐ *The Gift of the Crocodile: A Cinderella Story* **(Spice Islands, Sierra)** by Judy Sierra/ Reynold Ruffins

☐ *Abadeha: The **Philippine** Cinderella* by Myrna J. de la Paz/ Youshan Tang

☐ *The Way Meat Loves Salt: A Cinderella Tale from the **Jewish** Tradition* by Nina Jaffe/ Louise August

☐ *Jouanah: A **Hmong** Cinderella* by Jewell Reinhard Coburn/Tzexa Cherta Lee/Anne Sibley O'Brien

☐ *The Turkey Girl: A **Zuni** Cinderella Story* by Penny Pollack/ Ed Young

☐ *Cendrillon: A **Caribbean** Cinderella* by Robert San Souci/ Brian Pinkney

☐ *Cendrillon:* A **Cajun** Cinderella *by Sheila Hebert Collins/ Patrick Soper*

☐ *Mufaro's Beautiful Daughters: An **African** Tale* by John Steptoe

☐ *Cindy Ellen: A **Wild Western** Cinderella* by Susan Lowell/ Jane Manning

☐ *The **Irish** Cinderlad* by Shirley Climo/ Ruth Heller

☐ *Fair, Brown and Trembling: An **Irish** Cinderella Story* by Jude Daly

☐ *Joe Cinders* by Marianne Mitchell/Ryan Langdo

☐ *Prince Cinders* by Babette Cole

☐ *Cinder Edna* by Ellen Jackson/ Kevin O'Malley

☐ *Cinder-Elly* by Frances Minters and illustrated by G. Brian Karas

☐ *Bigfoot Cinderrrrrella* by Tony Johnston and illustrated by James Warhola

☐ _____

☐ _____

Civil War

☐ *The Blue and the Gray* by Eve Bunting/ Ned Bittinger

☐ *The Gettysburg Address* by Abraham Lincoln/ Michael McCurdy

☐ *Pink and Say* by Patricia Polacco

☐ *Jim Limber Davis: A Black Orphan in the Confederate White House* by Rickey Pittman/ Judith Hierstein

☐ *The Legend of Old Abe: A Civil War Eagle* by Kathy-Jo Wargin/ Laurie Caple

☐ *Willie McLean and the Civil War Surrender* by Candice Ransom/ Jeni Reeves

☐ *Silent Witness* by Robin Friedman/ Claire A. Nivola

☐ *Cassie's Sweet Berry Pie: A Civil War Story* by Karen B. Winnick

☐ *Mr. Lincoln's Whiskers* by Karen B. Winnick

☐ *Hold the Flag High* by Catherine Clinton/ Shane W. Evans

☐ *The Story of the H.L. Hunley and Queenie's Coin* by Fran Hawk/ Dan Nance

☐ *The Last Brother: A Civil War Tale* by Trinka Hakes Noble/ Robert Papp

☐ _____

☐ _____

கைகைகைகை ஒஒஒஒ

Dancing Bliss

☐ *Isadora Dances* by Rachel Isadora

☐ *I Dreamed I was a Ballerina* by Anna Pavlova/ Edgar Degas

☐ *Jose! Born to Dance: The Story of Jose Limon* by Susanna Reich/ Raul Colon

☐ *My Mama Had a Dancing Heart* by Libba Gray/ Raul Colon

☐ *Ballet of the Elephants* by Leda Schubert/ Robert Andrew Parker

☐ *The Nutcracker Ballet* by Vladimir Vagin

☐ *Coppelia* by Margot Fonteyn/ Steve Johnson/ Lou Fancher

☐ *Swan Lake* by Margot Fonteyn/ Peter Ilich Tchaikovsky/ Trina Schart Hyman

☐ *Lili at Ballet* by Rachel Isadora

☐ *Song and Dance Man* by Karen Ackerman/ Stephen Gammell

☐ *The Dance* by Richard Paul Evans/ Jonathan Linton

☐ *Dancing in the Wings* by Debbie Allen/ Kadir Nelson

☐ _____

☐ _____

In the World of Dolls

☐ *The Ticky-Tacky Doll* by Cynthia Rylant/ Harvey Stevenson

☐ *Dahlia* by Barbara McClintock

☐ *Elisabeth* by Claire A. Nivola

☐ *Little Kim's Doll* by Kim Yaroshevskaya/ Luc Melanson

☐ *The Last Doll* by Diane Gonzales Bertrand/ Anthony Accardo

☐ *Sophie and Rose* by Kathryn Lasky/ Wendy Anderson Halperin

☐ *Babushka's Doll* by Patricia Polacco

☐ *Fairy Houses* by Tracy Kane

☐ *The Chalk Doll* by Charlotte Pomerantz/ Frane Lessac

☐ *The Apple Doll* by Elisa Kleven

☐ *A Doll Named Dora Anne* by Yona Zeldis McDonough/ DyAnne DiSalvo

☐ *The Dolls' Christmas* by Tasha Tudor

☐ *The Never-Forgotten Doll* by Lisa McCourt/ Mary O'Keef Young

☐ *Elizabeti's Doll* by Stephanie Stuve-Bodeen/ Christy Hale

☐ *La La Rose* by Satomi Ichikawa

☐ *Trouble Dolls* by Jimmy & Savannah Buffett/ Lambert Davis

☐ *Almost to Freedom* by Vaunda Micheaux Nelson/ Colin Bootman

☐ *The Tale of Two Bad Mice* by Beatrix Potter

☐ *The Magic Nesting Doll* by Jacqueline K. Ogburn/ Laurel Long

☐ *Sasha's Matrioshka Dolls* by Jana Dillon/ Deborah Lattimore

☐ *The Littlest Matryoshka* by Corine Demas Bliss/ Kathryn Brown

☐ *The Wooden Doll* by Susan Bonners

☐ *Debbie's Dollhouse* by Barbara Kunz Loots/ Pat Paris

☐ *The Gingerbread Doll* by Susan Tews/ Megan Lloyd

☐ *The Very Best Doll* by Julia Noonan

☐ *The China Doll* by Elza Pilgrim/ Carmen Segovia

☐ *Mud Pies and Other Recipes: A Cookbook for Dolls* by Marjorie Winslow/ Erik Blegvad

☐ _____

☐ _____

202

Fairy Tales & Folktales

☐ *The Magic Fish* by Freya Littledale

☐ *Puss-in-Boats* by Charles Perrault and Fred Marcellino

☐ *Little Red Riding Hood* by Trina Schart Hyman

☐ *Merlin and the Making of the King* by Trina Schart Hyman

☐ *The Kitchen Knight* by Trina Schart Hyman

☐ *St. George and the Dragon* by Margaret Hodges and Trina Schart Hyman

☐ *Goldilocks and the Three Bears* by Jan Brett

☐ *Gingerbread Baby* by Jan Brett

☐ *Town Mouse, Country Mouse* by Jan Brett

☐ *Goldilocks* by Jan Brett

☐ *The Wild Swans* by Hans Christian Andersen/ Naomi Lewis / Anne Yvonne Gilbert

☐ *Rapunzel* by Paul O. Zelinsky

☐ *Rumpelstiltskin* by Paul O. Zelinsky

☐ *Hansel and Gretel* by Rika Lesser and Paul O. Zelinsky

☐ *Sleeping Beauty* by K.Y. Craft

☐ *The Secret-Keeper* by Kate Coombs/ Heather M. Solomon

☐ *The Twelve Dancing Princesses* by Marianna Mayer and K.Y. Craft

☐ *Swamp Angel* by Anne Isaacs and Paul O. Zelinsky

☐ *Pecos Bill* by Steven Kellogg

☐ *John Henry* by Julius Lester and Jerry Pinkney

☐ *King Midas and the Golden Touch* by Charlotte Craft and K.Y. Craft

☐ *The White Cat* by Robert D. San Souci

☐ *Mother Holly* by John Warren Stewig

☐ *Cinderella* by Ruth Sanderson

☐ *Papa Gatto: An Italian Fairy Tale* by Ruth Sanderson

☐ *Rose Red and Snow White* by Ruth Sanderson

☐ *Snow White and Rose Red* by Barbara Cooney

☐ *The Story of Little Black Sambo* by Helen Bannerman

☐ *The Adventures of Tom Thumb* by Marianna Mayer/ K.Y. Craft

☐ *Princess and the Kiss* by Jennie Bishop

☐ *The Squire and the Scroll* by Jennie Bishop

☐ *The Red Heels* by Robert D. San Souci/ Gary Kelley

☐ *Dona Flor: A Tall Tale about a Giant Woman with a Great Big Heart* by Pat Mora/ Raul Colon

☐ *The Twelve Dancing Princesses* by Marianna Mayers/ K.Y. Craft

☐ *Baba Yaga and Vasilisa the Brave* by Marianna Mayer/ K.Y. Craft

☐ *The Golden Heart of Winter* by Marilyn Singer/ Robert Rayevsky

☐ *The Talking Eggs* by Robert D. San Souci/ Jerry Pinkney

☐ *The Wild Swans* by Hans Christian Andersen/ Naomi Lewis/ Anne Yvonne Gilbert

☐ *Thumbelina* by Hans Christian Andersen/ Lauren Mills

☐ *The Well at the End of the World* by Robert D. San Souci/ Rebecca Walsh

☐ *The Magic Crystal* by Brigitte Weninger/ Robert Ingpen

☐ *The Golden Goose* by Brothers Grimm/ Uri Shulevitz

☐ *Tattercoats* by Joseph Jacobs/ Margot Tomes

☐ *The Wishing of Biddy Malone* by Joy Cowley/ Christopher Denise

☐ *The Bee-Man of Orn* by Frank R. Stockton/ P.J. Lynch

☐ *Juan Verdades: The Man who Couldn't Tell a Lie* by Joe Hayes/ Joseph Daniel Fiedler

☐ *Coyote: A Trickster Tale from the American Southwest* by Gerald McDermott

☐ *Raven: A Trickster Tale from the Pacific* by Gerald McDermott

☐ *Zomo the Rabbit: A Trickster Tale from West Africia* by Gerald McDermott

☐ *Jubuti the Tortoise: A Trickster Tale from the Amazon* by Gerald McDermott

☐ _____

☐ _____

Gardening Treasures

☐ *The Secret Garden* by Frances Hodgson Burnett/ Karen Prichett

☐ *From Seed to Plant* by Gail Gibbons

☐ *Holly Bloom's Garden* by Sarah Ashman/ Nancy Parent/ Lori Mitchell

☐ *Planting a Rainbow* by Lois Ehlert

☐ *Jack's Garden* by Henry Cole

☐ *Grandma's Garden* by Elaine Moore/ Dan Andreasen

☐ *Miss Rumphius* by Barbara Cooney

☐ *A Packet of Seeds* by Deborah Hopkinson/ Bethanne Andersen

☐ *The Tiny Seed* by Eric Carle

☐ *Sunflower House* by Eve Bunting/ Kathryn Hewitt

☐ *Sunflower Sal* by Janet S. Anderson/ Elizabeth Johns

☐ *Camille and the Sunflowers* by Laurence Anholt

☐ _____

☐ _____

In Conversation with God

☐ *When Daddy Prays* by Nikki Grimes/ Tim Ladwig

☐ *The Wonderful Happens* by Cynthia Rylant/ Coco Dowley

☐ *The Tale of Three Trees* by Angela Elwell Hunt/ Tim Jonke

☐ *The Giving Tree* by Shel Silverstein

☐ *Jesus* by Brian Wildsmith

☐ *The Lord's Prayer* by Tim Ladwig

☐ *Morning has Broken* by Eleanor Parjeon/ Tim Ladwig

☐ *Glory* by Nancy White Carlstrom/ Debra Reid Jenkins

☐ *The Monk Who Grew in Prayer* by Claire Brandenbur

☐ *All Things Bright and Beautiful* by Cecil Frances Alexander/ Bruce Whatley

☐ *On Morning Wings* by Reeve Linbergh/ Holly Meade

☐ *The Circle of Days* by Reeve Linbergh/ Cathie Felstead

☐ _____

☐ _____

(Books by Max Lucado)

☐ *Just in Case You Ever Wonder* illustrated by Toni Goffe

☐ *You are Special* illustrated by Sergio Martinez

☐ *You are Mine* illustrated by Sergio Martinez

☐ *Just the Way You Are* illustrated by Sergio Martinez

☐ *Best of All* illustrated by Sergio Martinez

☐ *Coming Home* illustrated by Justin Gerard

☐ *Because I Love You* illustrated by Mitchell Heinze

☐ *Small Gifts in God's Hand* illustrated by Cheri Bladholm

☐ *The Children of the King* illustrated by Toni Goffe

☐ *The Crippled Lamb* illustrated by Liz Bonham

☐ _____

☐ _____

The Great Depression

☐ *Saving Strawberry Farm* by Deborah Hopkinson/ Rachel Isadora

☐ *Leah's Pony* by Elizabeth Friedrich/ Michael Garland

☐ *The Bravest of Us All* by Marsha Diane Arnold/ Brad Sneed

☐ *Potato: A Tale from the Great Depression* by Kate Lied/ Lisa Campbell Ernst

☐ *Dust for Dinner* by Ann Turner/ Robert Barrett

☐ *Hannah and the Perfect Picture Pony* by Sara Goodman Zimet/ Sandy Ferguson Fuller

☐ *Finding Daddy* by Jo Harper/ Josephine Harper/ Ron Mazellan

☐ *Angels in the Dust* by Margot Theis Raven/ Roger Essley

☐ *The Dust Bowl* by David Booth/ Karen Reczuch

☐ _____

☐ _____

Home Sweet Home

☐ *Let's Go Home: The Wonderful Things about a House* by Cynthia Rylant/ Wendy Anderson Halperin

☐ *Our Old House* by Susan Vizurraga/ Leslie Baker

☐ *The Little House* by Virginia Lee Burton

☐ *Homeplace* by Anne Shelby/ Wendy Anderson Halperin

☐ *All the Places to Love* by Patricia MacLachlan/ Michael Wimmer

☐ *Home Place* by Crescent Dragonwagon/ Jerry Pinkney

☐ *It Could Always be Worse* by Margot Zemach

☐ *Always Room for One More* by Sorche Nic Leodhas/ Nonny Hogrogian

☐ *We were Tired of Living in a House* by Liesel Moak Skorpen/ Joe Cepeda

☐ _____

☐ _____

Immigration Booklist

☐ *Watch the Stars Come Out* by Riki Levinson/ Diane Goode

☐ *A Very Important Day* by Maggie Rugg Herold/ Catherine Stock

☐ *Ellis Island* by Lori Mortensen/ Matthew Skeens

☐ *Angel Island* by Lori Mortensen/ Matthew Skeens

☐ *Oranges on Golden Mountain* by Elizabeth Partridge/ Aki Sogabe

☐ *Buba Leah and her Paper Children* by Lillian Hammer Ross/ Mary Morgan-Vanroyen

☐ *Maggie's Amerikay* by Barbara Timberlake Russell/ Jim Burke

☐ *One Green Apple* by Eve Bunting/ Ted Lewin

☐ *Tattered Sails* by Verla Kay/ Dan Andreasen

☐ *Coming to America: The Story of Immigration* by Betsy Maestro/ Susannah Ryan

☐ *Dreaming of America: An Ellis Island Story* by Eve Bunting/ Ben F. Stahl

☐ *Silent Movie* by Avi/ C.B. Mordan

☐ *At Ellis Island: A History in Many Voices* by Louise Peacock/ Walter Lyon Krudop

☐ *Escaping to America: A True Story* by Rosalyn Schanzer

☐ *The Butterfly Seeds* by Mary Watson

☐ *When Jessie Came Across the Sea* by Amy Hest/ P.J. Lynch

☐ *The Memory Coat* by Elvira Woodruff/ Michael Dooling

☐ *The Dream Jar* by Bonnie Pryor/ Mark Graham

☐ *Grandmother and the Runaway Shadow* by Liz Rosenberg/ Beth Peck

☐ *Small Beauties* by Elvira Woodruff/ Adam Rex

☐ *Immigrant Girl* by Brett Harvey/ Deborah Kogan Ray

☐ *Show Way* by Jacqueline Woodson/ Hudson Talbott

☐ *The Trip Back Home* by Janet S. Wong/ Bo Jia

☐ *Annushka's Voyage* by Edith Tarbescu/ Lydia Dabcovich

☐ *Together in Pinecone Patch* by Thomas F. Yezerski

☐ *Journey to Ellis Island* by Carol Bierman/ Laurie Mcgaw

☐ *Grandfather's Journey* by Allen Say

☐ *Tea with Milk* by Allen Say

☐ *Love as Strong as Ginger* by Lenore Look/ Stephen T. Johnson

☐ *Hiromi's Hands* by Lynne Barasch

☐ *A Day's Work* by Eve Bunting/ Ronald Himler

☐ *If Your Name was Changed at Ellis Island* by Ellen Levine/ Wayne Parmenter

☐ *Faraway Home* by Jane Kurtz/ E.B. Lewis

☐ *Marianthe's Story: Painted Words and Spoken Memories* by Aliki

☐ *A Picnic in October* by Eve Bunting/ Nancy Carpenter

☐ *Landed* by Milly Lee/ Yangsook Choi

☐ *Kai's Journey to Gold Mountain* by Katrina Saltonstall Currier/ Gabhor Utomo

☐ *They were Strong and Good* by Robert Lawson

☐ *The Silence in the Mountains* by Liz Rosenberg/ Chris K. Soentpiet

☐ *Journey Home* by Lawrence McKay, Jr./ Dom and Keunhee Lee

☐ *Two Mrs. Gibsons* by Toyomi Igus/ Daryl Wells

☐ *The Color of Home* by Mary Hoffman/ Karen Littlewood

☐ *Rebekkah's Journey* by Ann E. Burg/ Joel Iskowitz

☐ *An Ellis Island Christmas* by Maxinne Rhea Leighton/ Dennis Nolan

☐ *Junk Man's Daughter* by Sonia Levitin/ Guy Forfirio

☐ _____

☐ _____

Indian Lore

☐ *Legend of the Indian Paintbrush* by Tomie dePaola

☐ *The Legend of the Bluebonnet* by Tomie dePaola

☐ *Arrow to the Sun: A Pueblo Indian Tale* by Gerald DcDermott

☐ *Moonstick: The Seasons of the Sioux* by Eve Bunting/ John Sandford

☐ *Corn is Maize: The Gift of the Indians* by Aliki

☐ *Love Flute* by Paul Goble

☐ *Broken Feather* by Verla Kay/ Stephen Alcorn

☐ *Thirteen Moons on Turtle's Back* by Joseph Bruchac/ Thomas Locker

☐ *The Earth under Sky Bear's Feet* by Joseph Bruchac/ Thomas Locker

☐ *The Mud Pony* by Caron Lee Cohen/ Shonto Begay

☐ *Crazy Horse's Vision* by Joseph Bruchac/ S.D. Nelson

☐ *The Star People* by S.D. Nelson

☐ *Gift Horse* by S.D. Nelson

214

☐ *Mystic Horse* by Paul Goble

☐ *Her Seven Brothers* by Paul Goble

☐ *Star Boy* by Paul Goble

☐ *Buffalo Woman* by Paul Goble

☐ *The Gift of the Sacred Dog* by Paul Goble

☐ *Crow Chief* by Paul Goble

☐ *Heetunka's Harvest: A Tale of the Plain Indians* by Jennifer Berry Jones/ Shannon Keegan

☐ *My Life with the Indians* by Robin Moore/ Victor Ambrus

☐ *Malian's Song* by Marge Bruchac/ William Maughan

☐ *A Boy Called Slow* by Joseph Bruchac/ Rocco Baviera

☐ *Shota and the Star Quilt* by Margaret Bateson-Hill

☐ *The Buffalo Jump* by Peter Roop/ Bill Farnsworth

☐ *The Magic of Spider Woman* by Lois Duncan/ Shonto Begay

☐ *The Rough-Faced Girl: An Algonquin Indian Cinderella* by Rafe Martin/ David Shannon

☐ *Doesn't Fall off His Horse* by Virginia A. Stroud

☐ *The Legend of the Lady's Slipper* by Kathy-Jo Wargin/ Gijsbert van Frankenhuyzen

☐ *Sequoyah* by James Rumford

☐ *The Legend of Blue Jacket* by Michael P. Spradlin/Ronald Himler

☐ *Dancing with the Indians* by Angela Shelf Medearis/

Constance Marshall

☐ *The First Strawberries* by Joseph Bruchac/ Anna Vojtech

☐ *How the Stars Fell into the Sky: A Navajo Legend* by Jerrie Oughton/ Lisa Desimini

☐ *Gray Wolf's Search* by Bruce Swanson/ Gary Peterson

☐ *The Land of Gray Wolf* by Thomas Locker

☐ *People of the Breaking Day* by Marcia Sewall

☐ *When the Shadbush Blooms* by Carla Messinger/ Susan Katz/ David Kanietakeron Fadden

☐ *The Great Ball Game: A Muskogee Story* by Joseph Bruchac/ Susan L. Roth

☐ *Night Dancer* by Marcia Vaughan/ Lisa Desimini

☐ *Rainbow Crow* by Nancy Van Laan/ Beatriz Vidal

☐ *The Great Race* by Paul Goble

☐ *The Star Maiden: An Ojibway Tale* by Barbara Juster Esbensen/ Helen K. Davie

☐ _____

☐ _____

✺✺✺✺ ✺✺✺✺

216

Libraries and Books

☐ *Library Lion* by Michelle Knudsen/ Kevin Hawkes

☐ *The Library* by Sarah Stewart/ David Small

☐ *Book! Book! Book!* By Deborah Bruss/ Tiphanie Beeke

☐ *The Inside-Outside Book of Libraries* by Roxie Munro/ Julia Cummins

☐ *The Librarian Who Measured the Earth* by Kathryn Lasky

☐ *The Librarian of Basra* by Jeanette Winter

☐ *Miss Smith's Incredible Storybook* by Michael Garland

☐ *Wild about Books* by Judy Sierra/ Marc Brown

☐ *Aunt Chip and the Great Triple Creek Dam Affair* by Patricia Polacco

☐ *"L" is for Library* by Sonya Terry/ Nicole Wong

☐ *"B" is for Bookworm: A Library Alphabet* by Anita C. Prieto/ Renee Graef

☐ *The Shelf Elf with Library Lessons* by Jackie Hopkins/ Rebecca Thornburgh

☐ *Richard Wright and the Library Card* by William Miller/ Gregory Christie

☐ *Jay and the Bounty of Books* by Randall Ivey/ Chuck Galey

☐ *The Library Dragon* by Carmen Agra Deedy/ Michael P. White

☐ *Stella Louella's Runaway Book* by Lisa Campbell Ernst

☐ *The Library of Alexandria* by Kelly Trumble/ Robina MacIntyre Marshall

☐ *Library Lil* by Suzanne Williams/ Steven Kellogg

☐ *Tomas and the Library Lady* by Pat Mora/ Raul Colon

☐ *The Old Woman Who Loved to Read* by John Winch

☐ *A Library for Juana* by Pat Mora/ Beatriz Vidal

☐ *Goin' Somplace Special* by Patricia C. McKissack/ Jerry Pinkney

☐ *Please Bury Me in the Library* by J. Patrick Lewis/ Kyle M. Stone

☐ *The Boy Who was Raised by Librarians* by Carla Morris/ Brad Sneed

☐ *Marguerite Makes a Book* by Bruce Robertson/ Kathryn Hewitt

☐ *Caedmon's Song* by Ruth Ashby/ Bill Slavin

☐ *The Incredible Book Eating Boy* by Oliver Jeffers

☐ *The Hard-Times Jar* by Ethel Footman Smothers/ John

Holyfield

☐ *Johann Gutenberg and the Amazing Printing Press* by Bruce Koscielniak/

☐ *Across a Dark & Wild Sea* by Don Brown/ Deborah Nadel

☐ _____

☐ _____

Music

☐ *Caedmon Song* by Ruth Ashby/ Bill Slavin

☐ *Pages of Music* by Tony Johnston/ Tomie dePaola

☐ *Mozart Finds a Melody* by Stephen Costanza

☐ *Mozart Tonight* by Julie Downing

☐ *Musicians of the Sun* by Gerald McDermott

☐ *Zin! Zin! Zin! A Violin* by Lloyd Moss/ Marjorie Priceman

☐ *Bach's Big Adventure* by Sallie Ketcham/ Timothy Bush

☐ *Meet the Orchestra* by Ann Hayes/ Karmen Thompson

☐ *The Story of the Incredible Orchestra* by Bruce Koscielniak

☐ *Ah, Music!* by Aliki

☐ *Two Scarlet Songbirds: A Story of Anton Dvorak* by Carole Lexa Schaefer/ Elizabeth Rosen

☐ *The Philharmonic Gets Dressed* by Karla Kuskin/ Marc Simont

☐ *The Cello of Mr. O* by Jane Cutler/ Greg Couch

☐ *M is for Music* by Kathleen Krull/ Stacy Innerst

☐ *M is for Melody* by Kathy-jo Wargin/ Katherine Larson

☐ *Peter and the Wolf* by Vladimir Vagin

☐ *Music for the End of Time* by Jennifer Bryant/ Beth Peck

☐ *Grateful: A Song of Giving Thanks* by John Bucchino/ Anna-Liisa Hakkarainen

☐ *Silent Night: The Song and its Story* by Margaret Hodges/ Tim Ladwig

☐ _____

☐ _____

Appreciating Nature

☐ *Anna's Table* by Eve Bunting/ Taia Morley

☐ *The Quiet Place* by Douglas Wood/ Dan Andreasen

☐ *Treasures of the Heart* by Alice Ann Miller/ K. L. Darnell

☐ *Cactus Hotel* by Brenda Z. Guiberson/ Megan Lloyd

☐ *Grandfather Twilight* by Barbara Helen Berger

☐ *Miss Rumphius* by Barbara Cooney

☐ *Henry David's House* by Henry David Thoreau/ Peter Riore

☐ *Night in the Country* by Cynthia Rylant/ Mary Szilagyi

☐ *Creatures of Earth, Sea, and Sky* by Georgia Heard/ Jennifer Owings Dewey

☐ *Birds in Your Backyard* by Barbara Herket

☐ *Louisa May and Mr. Thoreau's Flute* by Julie Dunlap/ Marybeth Lorbeicki/ Mary Azarian

☐ *Canoe Days* by Gary Paulsen/ Ruth Wright Paulsen

☐ *Henry David's House* by Henry David Thoreau/ Steven Schnur/ Peter M. Fiore

☐ *Walking with Henry: Based on the Life and Works of Henry David Thoreau* by Thomas Locker

☐ *Into the Woods* by Robert Burleigh/ Wendell Minor

☐ *John Muir: America's Naturalist* by Thomas Locker/ Edgar Wayburn

☐ *Each Living Thing* by Joanne Ryder/ Ashley Wolff

☐ *All the Places to Love* by Patricia MacLachlan/ Michael Wimmer

☐ *A Packet of Seeds* by Deborah Hopkinson/ Bethanne Andersen

☐ *Cloud Dance* by Thomas Locker

☐ *One Small Square Series* by Donald M. Silver/ Patricia Wynne

☐ *The Salamander Room* by Anne Mazer/ Steve Johnson/ Lou Fancher

☐ *Crawdad Creek* by Scott Russell Sanders/ Robert Hynes

☐ *Fun with Nature: Take-Along Guide* by Mel Boring

☐ *Crinkleroot's Guides* by Jim Arnosky

☐ *In the Fiddle is a Song* by Durga Bernhard

☐ _____

☐ _____

Picnic and Family Reunions

☐ *We had a Picnic this Sunday Past* by Jacqueline Woodson/ Diane Greenseid

☐ *The Relatives Came* by Cynthia Rylant/ Stephen Gammell

☐ *The Keeping Quilt* by Patricia Polocca

☐ *Picnic* by Emily Arnold McCully

☐ *Jubilee* by Ellen Yeomans/ Tim Ladwig

☐ *Picnic at Mudsock Meadow* by Patricia Polocca

☐ *Grandpa's Hotel* by Riki Levinson/ David Soman

☐ *Homeplace* by Anne Shelby/ Wendy Anderson Halperin

☐ *Old Home Town* by Donald Hall/ Emily Arnold McCully

☐ *Someone's Coming to Our House* by Kathi Appelt/ Nancy Carpenter

☐ *Song and Dance Man* by Karen Ackerman/ Stephen Gammell

☐ *Rattlebang Picnic* by Margaret Mahy/ Steven Kellog

☐ *When Lightning Comes in a Jar* by Patricia Polocca

☐ *Tanya's Reunion* by Valerie Flournoy/ Jerry Pinkney

☐ *The Visit* by Reeve Lindbergh/ Wendy Halperin

☐ *The Most Perfect Spot* by Diane Goode

☐ _____

☐ _____

Pioneers & Westward Movement

☐ *Araminta's Paint Box* by Karen Ackerman/ Betsy Lewin

☐ *Going West* by Jean Van Leeuwen/ Thomas B. Allen

☐ *Dandelions* by Eve Bunting/ Greg Shed

☐ *Grandma Essie's Covered Wagon* by David Williams/ Wikdor Sadows

☐ *Going West* by Laura Ingalls Wilder/ Renee Graef

☐ *Prairie Day* by Laura Ingalls Wilder/ Renee Graef

☐ *The Way West* by Amelia Stewart Knight/ Michael McCurdy

☐ *Prairie Christmas* by Brett Harvey/ Deborah Kogan Ray

☐ *Apples to Oregon* by Deborah Hopkinson/ Nancy

224

Carpenter

☐ *Aurora Means Dawn* by Scott Russell Sanders/ Jill Kastner

☐ *My Floating House* by Scott Russell Sanders/ Helen Cogancherry

☐ *Pappy's Handkerchief* by Devin Scillian/ Chris Ellison

☐ *Sunsets of the West* by Tony Johnston/ Ted Lewin

☐ *Covered Wagons, Bumpy Trails* by Verla Kay/ S.D. Schindler

☐ *Homespun Sarah* by Verla Kay/ Ted Rand

☐ _____

☐ _____

Quilting with Books

☐ *Quilting Now & Then* by Karen B. Willing/ Julie B. Dock/ Sarah Morse

☐ *Quilt of Dreams* by Mindy Dwyer

☐ *Quilt Block History of Pioneer Days* by Mary Cobb

☐ *The Moon Quilt* by Sunny Warner

☐ *Show Way* by Jacqueline Woodson/ Hudson Talbott

☐ *Papa and the Pioneer Quilt* by Jean Van Leeuwen/ Rebecca Bond

☐ *Reuben and the Quilt* by Merle Good, P. Buckley Moss

☐ *Oma's Quilt* by Paulette Bourgeois/ Stephane Jorisch

☐ *The Quilt* by Ann Jonas

☐ *The Quilt Story* by Tony Johnston/ Tomie dePaola

☐ *The Patchwork Quilt* by Valerie Flournoy/ Jerry Pinkney

☐ *Sweet Clara and the Freedom Quilt* by Deborah Hopkinson/ James Ransome

☐ *Selina and the Bear Paw Quilt* by Barbara Smucker / Janet Wilson

☐ *Sunflower Sal* by Janet S. Anderson/ Elizabeth Johns

☐ *The Keeping Quilt* by Patricia Polacco

☐ *Martha Ann's Quilt for Queen Victoria* by Kyra E. Hicks/ Lee Edward Fodi

☐ *The Name Quilt* by Phyllis Root/ Margot Apple

☐ *Eight Hands Round: A Patchwork Alphabet* by Ann Whitford Paul/ Jeanette Winter

☐ *Sam Johnson and the Blue Ribbon Quilt* by Lisa Campbell Ernst

☐ *The Josefina Story Quilt* by Eleanor Coerr/ Bruce Degen

☐ *The Patchwork Lady* by Mary K. Whittington/ Jane Dyer/ Jane Yolen

☐ *The Quiltmaker's Gift* by Jeff Brumbeau/ Gail De Marcken

☐ *Bringing the Farmhouse Home* by Gloria Whelan/ Jada Rowland

☐ *The Promise Quilt* by Candice F. Ransom/ Ellen Beier

☐ *The Dream Quilt* by Celeste Ryan/ Mary Haverfield

☐ *The Tamale Quilt* by Jane Tenorio-Coscarelli

☐ *The Tortilla Quilt* by Jane Tenorio-Coscarelli

☐ *A Quilt for Baby* by Kim Lewis

☐ *The Secret to Freedom* by Marcia Vaughan/ Larry Johnson

☐ *A Name on the Quilt: A Story of Remembrance* Jeannine Atkins/ Tad Hills

☐ *Grandpa's Quilt* by Betsy Franco/ Linda Bild

☐ *Luka's Quilt* by Georgia Guback

☐ *Cassie's Word Quilt* by Faith Ringgold

☐ *Pieces: A Year in Poems and Quilts* by Anna Grossnickle Hines

☐ *Under the Quilt of Night* by Deborah Hopkinson/ James E. Ransome

☐ *The Rag Coat* by Lauren Mills

☐ *The Pumpkin Blanket* by Deborah Turney Zagwyn

☐ *Shota and the Star Quilt* by Margaret Bateson-Hill

☐ _____

☐ _____

Rain Dance

☐ *Hurricane Wolf* by Diane Paterson

☐ *Hurricane* by David Wiesner

☐ *Time of Wonder* by Robert McCloskey

☐ *Water Dance* by Thomas Locker

☐ *A Drop around the World* by Barbara McKinney/ Michael S. Maydak

☐ *The Drop Goes Plop* by Sam Godwin/ Simone Abel

☐ *Rain* by Peter Spier

☐ *Rain, Drop, Splash* by Alvin Tresselt/ Leonard Weisgard

☐ *Bringing the Rain to Kapiti Plain* by Verna Aardema/ Beatriz Vidal

☐ *Down Comes the Rain* by Franklyn Mansfield Branley/ James Graham Hale

☐ *Come on, Rain!* by Karen Hesse/ Jon J. Muth

☐ *Burt Dow, Deep-Water Man* by Robert McCloskey

☐ _____

Struggling Readers

☐ *Once Upon a Time* by Niki Daly

☐ *The Bee Tree* by Patricia Polacco

☐ *Thank you, Mr. Falker* by Patricia Polacco

☐ *Up the Learning Tree* by Marcia Vaughan/ Derek Blanks

☐ *Amber on the Mountain* by Tony Johnston/ Robert Duncan

☐ *Raising Sweetness* by Diane Stanley/ G. Brian Karas

☐ *More than Anything Else* by Marie Bradby/ Chris Soentpiet

☐ _____

☐ _____

Revolutionary War

☐ *The Boston Tea Party* by Steven Kroll/ Peter M. Fiore

☐ *Paul Revere's Midnight Ride* by Stephen Krensky/ Greg Harlin

☐ *They Call her Molly Pitcher* by Anne Rockwell/ Cynthia Von Buhler

☐ *Sybil's Night Ride* by Karen B. Winnick

☐ *Sleds on Boston Common* by Louise Borden/ Robert Andrew Parker

☐ *Katie's Trunk* by Ann Turner/ Ronald Himler

☐ *Charlotte* by Janet Lunn/ Brian Deines

☐ *Samuel's Choice* by Richard J. Berleth/ James Watling

☐ *When Washington Crossed the Delaware* by Lynne Cheney/ Peter M. Fiore

☐ *The Scarlet Stockings Spy* by Trinka Hakes Noble/ Robert Papp

☐ *Redcoats and Petticoats* by Katherine Kirkpatrick/ Ronald Himler

☐ *Hero on Horseback: The Story of Casimir Pulaski* by David R. Collins/ Larry Nolte

☐ *The Hatmaker's Sign* by Candace Fleming/ Robert Parker

☐ _____

☐ _____

September 11

☐ *The Man Who Walked Between the Towers* by Mordicai Gerstein

☐ *September 11, 2001: A Simple Account for Children* by Nancy Poffenberger/ Val Gottesman

☐ *The Little Chapel that Stood* by A.B. Curtiss

☐ *New York's Bravest* by Mary Pope Osborne/ Steve Johnson/ Lou Fancher

☐ *Fireboat: The Heroic Adventures of John J. Harvey* by Maira Kalman

☐ *Frankie Wonders…What Happened Today?* by Yvonne Conte

☐ _____

☐ _____

Shakespeare

☐ *Bard of Avon: The Story of William Shakespeare* by Diane Stanley/ Peter Vennema

☐ *William Shakespeare and the Globe* by Aliki

☐ *All the World's a Stage* by Rebecca Piatt Davidson/ Anita Lobel

☐ *William Shakespeare's MacBeth* by Bruce Coville/ Gary Kelley

☐ *Romero and Juliet* by Bruce Coville/ Dennis Nolan

☐ *Hamlet* by Bruce Coville/ Leonid Gore

- [ ] *Twelfth Night* by Bruce Coville/ Kathryn Hewitt
- [ ] *William Shakespeare's The Winter's Tale* by Bruce Coville/ LeUyen Pham
- [ ] *A Midsummer Night's Dream* by William Shakespeare/ Bruce Coville/ Dennis Nolan
- [ ] *Midsummer Night's Dream* by Eric Kincaid
- [ ] *William Shakespeare's The Tempest* by Bruce Coville/ Ruth Sanderson
- [ ] *The Tempest* by Marianna Mayer/ Lynn Bywaters
- [ ] *Shakespeare can be Fun series* by Lois Burdett
- [ ] *Bravo, Mr. William Shakespeare!* by Marcia Williams
- [ ] *Tales from Shakespeare* by Marcia Williams
- [ ] _____
- [ ] _____

Let it Snow

- [ ] *Katy and the Big Snow* by Virginia Lee Burton
- [ ] *The First Snow* by David Christiana
- [ ] *The Mitten* by Jan Brett

☐ *Dear Rebecca, Winter is Here* by Jean Craighead George/ Loretta Krupinski

☐ *When Winter Comes* by Nancy Van Laan/ Susan Gaber

☐ *First Snow* by Kim Lewis

☐ *The Snow Speaks* by Nancy White Carlstrom / Jane Dyer

☐ *Snow* by Uri Shulevitz

☐ *Too Many Mittens* by Florence & Louis Slobodkin

☐ *Robert's Snow* by Grace Lin

☐ *Children of the Northlights* by Ingri & Edgar D'Aulaire

☐ *The Big Snow* by Berta & Elmer Hader

☐ *The Snow Queen* by Hans Christian Anderson / Susan Jeffers

☐ *When will it Snow* by Bruce Hiscock

☐ *Sugar Snow* by Laura Ingalls Wilder/ Doris Ettlinger

☐ *White Snow, Bright Snow* by Alvin Tresselt / Roger Duvoisin

☐ *Snowflake Bentley* by Jacqueline Briggs Martin / Mary Azarian

☐ *Very Last First Time* by Jan Andrews / Ian Wallace

☐ *The Snowy Day* by Ezra Jack Keats (also on DVD)

☐ *Snowballs* by Lois Ehlert

☐ *Snow Crystals* by W. A. Bentley and W. J. Humphreys

☐ *My Brother Loved Snowflakes* by Mary Bahr / Laura Jacobsen

☐ *The Snowflake - A Water Cycle Story* by Neil Waldman

☐ *Snow Riders* by Constance McGeorge/ Mary Whyte

☐ *The Snowman* by Raymond Briggs

☐ *Snowmen at Night* by Caralyn Buehner/ Mark Buehner

☐ *Blizzard* by Carole Gerber/ Marty Husted

☐ *Dream Snow* by Eric Carle

☐ *The Last Snow of Winter* by Tony Johnston/ Friso Henstra

☐ *Winter Lullaby* by Barbara Seuling/ Greg Newbold

☐ *Geraldine's Big Snow* by Holly Keller

☐ _____

☐ _____

Summertime

☐ *Andrew Henry's Meadow* by Doris Burn

☐ *The Summerfolk* by Doris Burn

☐ *Grayboy* by Kay Chorao

☐ *Beach Day* by Karen Roosa/ Maggie Smith

☐ *Famous Seaweed Soup* by Antoinette Truglio Martin/ Nadine Bernard Westcott

☐ *To the Beach!* by Linda Ashman/ Nadine Bernard Westcott

☐ *Hattie and the Wild Waves* by Barbara Cooney

☐ *Clams All Year* by Maryann Cocca-Leffler

☐ *Time of Wonder* by Robert McCloskey

☐ *Beachcombing: Exploring the Seashore* by Jim Arnosky

☐ _____

☐ _____

Underground Railroad Booklist

☐ *Friend on Freedom River* by Gloria Whelan/ Gijsbert van Frankenhuyzen

☐ *Martha Ann's Quilt for Queen Victoria* by Kyra E. Hicks/ Lee Edward Fodi

☐ *Night Boat to Freedom* by Margot Theis Raven/ E.B. Lewis

☐ *The Secret to Freedom* by Marcia Vaughan/ Larry Johnson

☐ *The Patchwork Path: A Quilt Map to Freedom* by Bettye Stroud/ Erin Susanne Bennett

☐ *Henry's Freedom Box* by Ellen Levine/ Kadir Nelson

☐ *The Patchwork Quilt* by Valerie Flournoy/ Jerry Pinkney

☐ *From Slave Ship to Freedom Road* by Julius Lester/ Rod Brown

☐ *A Picture Book of Harriet Tubman* by David Adler

☐ *Minty: Story of Young Harriet Tubman* by Alan Schroeder/ Jerry Pinkney

☐ *Aunt Harriet's Underground Railroad in the Sky* by Faith Ringgold

☐ *Moses: When Harriet Tubman Led Her People to Freedom* by Carole Boston Weatherford/ Kadir Nelson

☐ *An Apple for Harriet Tubman* by Glennette Tilley Turner/ Susan Keeter

☐ *Almost to Freedom* by Vaunda Micheaux Nelson/ Colin Bootman

☐ *Sweet Clara and the Freedom Quilt* by Deborah Hopkinson/ James Ransome

☐ *Follow the Drinking Gourd* by Jeanette Winters

☐ *The Daring Escape of Ellen Craft* by Cathy Moore/ Mary O'Keefe Young

☐ *The Drinking Gourd* by F.N. Monjo/ Fred Brenner

☐ *Under the Quilt of Night* by Deborah Hopkinson/ James Ransome

☐ *Secret Signs: Escape through the Underground Railroad* by Anita Riggio

☐ *A Place Called Freedom* by Scott Russell Sanders

☐ *Crossing Bok Chitto* by Tim Tingle/ Jeanne Rorex Bridges

☐ *Allen Jay and the Underground Railroad* by Marlene Targ Brill/ Janice Lee Porter

☐ _____

☐ _____

(Older Readers)

☐ *If You Traveled on the Underground Railroad* by Ellen Levine/ Larry Johnson

☐ *The Last Safe House* by Barbara Greenwood/ Heather Collins

☐ *Amos Fortune, Free Man* by Elizabeth Yates

☐ _____

☐ _____

৵৵৵৵   ৵৵৵৵

Walk on the Wild Side ~ Camping/Hiking Books

☐ *The Lost Lake* by Allen Say

☐ *The Cabin Key* by Gloria Rand/ Ted Rand

☐ *Whistling* by Elizabeth Partridge/ Anna Grossnickle Hines

☐ *Stella & Roy Go Camping* by Ashley Wolff

☐ *Walking with Mama* by Barbara Stynes

☐ *Three Days on a River in a Red Canoe* by Vera B. Williams

☐ *When We Go Camping* by Margriet Ruurs/ Andrew Kiss

☐ *Toasting Marshmallows: Camping Poems* by Kate Kiesler/ Kristine O'Connell George

☐ *S is for Smores: A Camping Alphabet* by Helen Foster James/ Lita Judge

☐ *When Daddy Took Us Camping* by Julie Brillhart

☐ *When I Go Camping With Grandma* by Marion Dane Bauer/ Allen Garns

☐ *The Raft* by Jim Lamarche

☐ *Willie Takes a Hike* by Gloria Rand/ Ted Rand

☐ *Crinkleroot's Guide to Walking in Wild Places* by Jim Arnosky

☐ *Where Does the Trail Lead?* by Burton Albert/ J. Brian Pinkney

☐ *I Took a Walk* by Henry Cole

☐ *Nature Walk* by Douglas Florian

☐ *Walk When the Moon Is Full* by Francis Hamerstrom/ Robert Katona

☐ *Squish!: A Wetland Walk* by Nancy Luenn/ Ronald Himler

☐ *The Listening Walk* by Paul Showers/ Aliki

☐ *Night in the Country* by Cynthia Rylant/ Mary Szilagyi

☐ _____

☐ _____

Weather

☐ *Cloud Dance* by Thomas Locker

☐ *What will the Weather Be?* by Lynda Dewitt/ Carolyn Croll

☐ *Cloudy with a Chance of Meatballs* by Judi Barrett/ Ron Barrett

☐ *Weather Words and What They Mean* by Gail Gibbons

☐ *The Bravest of Us All* by Marsha Diane Arnold/ Brad Sneed

☐ *The Man Who Named the Clouds* by Julie Hannah/ Joan Holub/ Paige Billin-Frye

☐ _____

☐ _____

World War I

☐ *In Flanders Fields* by Linda Granfield/ Janet Wilson

☐ *Waiting for the Evening Star* by Rosemary Wells/ Susan Jeffers

☐ *Christmas in the Trenches* by John McCutcheon/ Henri Sorensen

☐ _____

☐ _____

World War II

☐ *Across the Blue Pacific* by Louise Borden/ Robert Andrew Parker

☐ *The Greatest Skating Race* by Louise Borden/ Niki Daly

☐ *The Little Ships* by Louise Borden/ Michael Foreman

☐ *Boxes for Katje* by Candace Fleming/ Stacey Dressen-McQueen

☐ *Star of Fear, Star of Hope* by Jo Hoestlandt/ Johanna Kang

☐ *Always Remember Me* by Marisabina Russo

☐ *Flowers on the Wall* by Miriam Nerlove

☐ *The Tuskegee Airmen Story* by Lynn M. Homan/ Thomas Reilly/ Rosalie M. Shepherd

☐ *The Lily Cupboard* by Shulamith Levey Oppenheim/ Ronald Himler

☐ *One Yellow Daffodil* by David A. Adler/ Lloyd Bloom

☐ *The Secret Seder* by Doreen Rappaport/ Emily Arnold McCully

☐ *The Feather-Bed Journey* by Paula Kurzband Feder/ Stacey Schuett

☐ *Erika's Story* by Ruth Vander Zee/ Roberto Innocenti

☐ *Rose Blanche* by Ian/ McEwan/ Roberto Innocenti/

☐ *The Harmonica* by Tony Johnston/ Ron Mazellan

☐ *The Cats in Krasinski Square* by Karen Hesse/ Wendy Watson

☐ *Faithful Elephants* by Yukio Tsuchiya/ Ted Lewin

☐ *The Yellow Star* by Carmen Agra Deedy/ Henri Sorensen

☐ *The Butterfly* by Patricia Polacco

☐ *Luba: The Angel of Bergen-Belsen* by Michelle Tryszynska-Frederick/ Ann Marshall

☐ *A Place Where Sunflowers Grew* by Amy Lee-Tai/ Felicia Hoshino

☐ *Mercedes and the Chocolate Pilot* by Margot Theis Raven/ Gijsbert van Frankenhuyzen

☐ *There Come a Soldier* by Peggy Mercer/ Ron Mazellan

☐ *One Candle* by Eve Bunting/ K. Wendy Popp

☐ *Music for the End of Time* by Jennifer Bryant/ Beth Peck

☐ *Lisette's Angel* by Amy Littlesugar/ Max Ginsburg

☐ *Wind Flyers* by Angela Johnson/ Loren Long

☐ *The Unbreakable Code* by Sara Hoagland Hunter/ Julia Miner

☐ *Baseball Saved Us* by Ken Mochizuki/ Dom Lee

☐ *The Bracelet* by Yoshiko Uchida/ Joanna Yardley

☐ *Pennies in a Jar* by Dori Chacones/ Ted Lewin

☐ *One Thousand Tracings* by Lita Judge

☐ *Rebekkah's Journey* by Ann E. Burg/ Joel Iskowitz

☐ *So Far From the Sea* by Eve Bunting/ Chris K. Soentpiet

☐ _____

☐ _____

Weaving

☐ *Weaving the Rainbow* by George Ella Lyon/ Stephanie Anderson

242

☐ *Charlie Needs a Cloak* by Tomie dePaola

☐ *The Goat in the Rug* by Charles Blood/ Martin Link/ Nancy Winslow Parker

☐ *The Chief's Blanket* by Michael Chanin/ Kim Howard

☐ *Red Berry Wool* by Robyn Eversole/ Tim Coffey

☐ *Argyle* by Barbara Brooks Wallace/ John Sandford

☐ *Warm as Wool* by Scott Russell Sanders/ Helen Cogancherry

☐ _____

☐ _____

(If you have any children books to contribute to the following lists or any lists that you would like to see developed, please contact the author. Her email can be found at http:caygibson.typepad.com)

A Christmas Tradition in Reading

What traditions will you share with your children or grandchildren this blessed season? The annual shopping trip to the mall to see Santa? The parties and caroling and trimming of the tree? Christmas feasting with relatives?

Well, I would like to offer you an idea for a different kind of feast—a feast of Christmas literature. Our family's favorite tradition is to experience the scents and glows, the warmth and love, the festivities and joy of Christmas through some very special books. Reading Advent and Christmas books is a wonderful way to remind our children of the true reason for the season—and to help all of us, parents and children alike, take a break from our frantic holiday "to do" list, and enjoy the real treasures of Christmas. I'd like to invite you and your family to join my family during this blessed season of Christmas in enjoying some good family reading. But first, you need to get properly prepared! Don't worry, though, this will be easy!

Once the children have donned their flannel pajamas and relaxed on the sofa with their pillows, bring out a bowl of buttery popcorn and mugs of hot cocoa. Turn off the overhead lights and snap on a dim lamp. This will relax the children and settle everyone down—including the family dog. As you begin to read, take a moment to look at your children's face as they fall under the spell of the story. Enjoy this time with them, and remember that you are giving them a gift that keeps on giving. These holiday stories will enrich your children's young lives (and yours) with a lovely memory that will live in their hearts and in their minds for many years to come.

Think about it this way . . . The Christmas toys will break and be forgotten. The shiny, crinkled Christmas paper will be thrown away. The Christmas feast will have disappeared, leaving behind a turkey carcass and pie crusts. Every celebration must come to an end—every one except the coming of Christ into our world and lives. Christmas literary treasures, and the memories they give your children, will ensure that the birth of Christ will be no passing event to them.

Because, there are so many wonderful Christmas books, it has been difficult to pick just a few to share. I hope my selections will encourage you to search for your own Christmas books and share them with your family.

Celebrate this beautiful season with a feast of holiday literature and start a new Advent tradition of reading with your children or grandchildren. This is one holiday tradition that is much simpler and less stressful than any other activity you do this year— and it is a gift that will keep on giving! So make sure there is a Christmas book under your tree this year.

෴෴෴෴   ෴෴෴෴

Christmas Booklist

This booklist contains some of my favorite Christmas titles and proves to be as endless as the starry skies. You'll have to reach down deep to the very toe of the stocking to see if more goodies are in there. A blank section has been added to include your favorite Christmas books that might not be found here. In that way, you can make it truly your own.

☐ *When It Snowed that Night* by Norma Farber/ Petra Mathers (a collection of Christmas poetry)

☐ *The Christmas Miracle of Jonathan Toomey* by Susan Wojciechowski/ P.J. Lynch

☐ *Country Angel Christmas* by Tomie dePaola

☐ *Waiting for Noel* by Ann Dixon/ Mark Graham

☐ *The Fir Tree* by Hans Christian Andersen

☐ *The Year of the Perfect Christmas Tree* by Gloria Houston/ Barbara Cooney

☐ *Christmas Tapestry* by Patricia Polacco

☐ *The Legend of the Candy Cane* by Lori Walburg/ James Bernardin

☐ *The Legend of the Poinsettia* by Tomie dePaola

☐ *The Legend of the Christmas Stocking* by Rick Osborne/ Jim Griffin

☐ *The Legend of the Christmas Tree* by Rick Osborne/ Bill Dodge

☐ *Silent Night: The Song and its Story* by Margaret Hodges/Tim Ladwig

☐ *The Little Match Girl* by Hans Christian Andersen/ Rachel Isadora or other various illustrators

☐ *Christmas in the Country* by Cynthia Rylant/ Diane Goode

☐ *The Nutcracker* (several adaptations and illustrated versions)

☐ *The Shoemaker's Dream* by Masahiro Kasuya/ Mildred Schell

☐ *A Small Miracle* by Peter Collington

☐ *The Christmas Candle* by Richard Paul Evans/ Jacob Collins

☐ *Why the Chimes Rang* by Raymond MacDonald Alden

☐ *The First Christmas Stocking* by Elizabeth Winthrop/ Bagram Ibatoulline

☐ *The Bears' Christmas Surprise* by Bruno Hachler/ Angela Kehlenbeck

☐ *The Christmas Coat* by Clyde Robert Bulla/ Sylvie Wickstrom

☐ *Jingle the Christmas Clown* by Tomie dePaola

☐ *The Twelve Days of Christmas* (various illustrated versions)

☐ *The Elves and the Shoemaker* by the Brother Grimm/ Jim LaMarche

☐ *December* by Eve Bunting/ David Diaz

☐ *The Gingerbread Doll* by Susan Tews/ Megan Lloyd

☐ *The Clown of God* by Tomie dePaola

☐ *Pages of Music* by Tony Johnston/ Tomie dePaola

☐ *How the Grinch Stole Christmas* by Dr. Seuss

☐ *Christmas Eve Blizzard* by Andrea Vlahakis/ Emanuel Schongut

☐ *The Cajun Night before Christmas* by James Rice

☐ *The Christmas Knight* by Jane Louise Curry/ Dyanne DiSalvo-Ryan

☐ *Good King Wenceslas* by John M. Neale/ Tim Ladwig

☐ *Stephen's Feast* by Jean Richardson/ Alice Englander

☐ *Christmas Tree Farm* by Ann Purmell/ Jill Weber

☐ *Prairie Christmas* by Elizabeth Van Steenwyk/ Ronald Himler

☐ *Santa's Favorite Story* by Hisako Aoki/ Ivan Gantschev

☐ *Yes, Virginia, There is a Santa Claus* by Francis P. Church/ Joel Spector

☐ *Santa Comes to Little House* by Laura Ingalls Wilder/ Renee Graef

☐ *The Polar Express* by Chris Van Allsburg

☐ *Saint Nicholas: The Real Story of the Christmas Legend* by Julie Steigemeyer/ Chris Ellison

☐ *Bear Stays Up for Christmas* by Karma Wilson/ Jane Chapman

☐ *The Legend of Papa Noel: A Cajun Christmas Story* by Terri Hoover Dunham/ Laura Knorr

☐ *The Miracle of Saint Nicholas* by Gloria Whelan/ Judith Brown

☐ *The Legend of Saint Nicholas* by Demi

☐ *The Legend of St. Nicholas: A Story of Christmas Giving* by Dandi Daley Mackall/Guy Porfirio

☐ *Angela and the Baby Jesus* by Frank McCourt/ Raul Colon

☐ *Great Joy* by Kate DiCamillo/ Bagram Ibatoulline

☐ *What Happened to Merry Christmas?* by Robert C. Baker/ Dave Hill

☐ *The Baker's Dozen: A Saint Nicholas Tale* by Aaron Shepard/ Wendy Edelson

☐ *The Baker's Dozen* by Heather Forest/ Susan Gaber

☐ *An Orange for Frankie* by Patricia Polacco

☐ *Silent Night* by Will Moses

☐ *The Twenty-Four Days before Christmas* by Madeleine L'Engle/ Joe DeVelasco

☐ *The Christmas Promise* by Susan Bartoletti/ David Christiana

☐ *One Christmas Dawn* by Candice Ransom/ Peter Fiore ☐ *Night Tree* by Eve Bunting

☐ *The Christmas Donkey* by Gillian McClure

☐ *Mortimer's Christmas Manger* by Karma Wilson/ Jan Chapman

☐ *To Hear the Angels Sing: A Christmas Poem* by W. Nikola-Lisa/ Jill Weber

☐ *The Donkey's Dream* by Barbara Helen Berger

☐ *The Crippled Lamb* by Max Lucado/ Liz Bonahm

☐ *The Tale of Three Trees* by Angela Elwell Hunt/ Tim Jonke

☐ *Who Was Born This Special Day?* by Eve Bunting

☐ *Mary Did You Know* by Mark Lowry

☐ *There was no Snow on Christmas Eve* by Pam Munoz Ryan/ Dennis Nolan

☐ *The Legend of the Christmas Rose* by William H. Hooks/ Richard Williams

☐ *When It Snowed that Night* by Norma Farber/ Petra Mathers (a collection of Christmas poetry)

☐ *Danny and the Kings* by Susan Cooper/ Jos. A. Smith

☐ *The Last Straw* by Fredrick H. Thury/ Vlasta van Kampen

☐ *Bright Christmas: An Angel Remembers* by Andrew Clements/ Kate Kiesler

☐ *Angels, Angels Everywhere* by Tomie dePaola

☐ *The Littlest Angel* by Charles Tazewell/ Deborah Lanino

Christmas around the World

☐ *Waiting for Christmas* by Kathleen Long Bostrom/ Alexi Natchev (Germany)

☐ *An Island Christmas* by Lynn Joseph/ Catherine Stock (Caribbean)

☐ *Christmas in Noisy Village* by Astrid Lindgren/ Ilon Wikland (Sweden)

☐ *Baboushka: A Christmas Folktale from Russia* by Arthur Scholey/ Helen Cann (Russia)

☐ *The Cajun Night before Christmas* by Trosclair/ James Rice (Louisiana)

☐ *The Night of Las Posadas* by Tomie dePaola (Mexico)

☐ *The Santero's Miracle* by Rudolfo Anaya/ Amy Cordova (New Mexico)

□ *Nine Days to Christmas* by Marie Hall Ets/ Aurora Labastida (Mexico)

□ *Too Many Tamales* by Gary Soto/ Ed Martinez (South America)

□ *The Huron Carol* illustrated by Frances Tyrrell (Huron Indian Tribe)

□ *Marta and the Manger Straw: A Christmas Tradition from Poland* by Virginia Kroll/ Robyn Belton (Poland)

□ *Lucia Morning in Sweden* by Ewa Rydaker (Sweden)

□ *Miracle of the Poinsettia* by Brian Cavanaugh/ Dennis Rockhill (Mexico)

□ *The Christmas Drum: A Romanian Christmas Custom* by Maureen Brett Hooper/ Diane Paterson (Romania)

□ *A Kenya Christmas* by Tony Johnston/ Leonard Jenkins (Africa)

□ *What's Cooking, Jamela?* by Niki Daly (South Africa)

For a more developed Christmas booklist; as well as featured books, annotations, recipes, and essays; you might want to check into *Christmas Mosaic: An Illustrated Book Study for Advent and Christmas* (published by Hillside Education www.hillsideeducation.com).

A Word from the Author:

Childhood is a time to climb trees, run across open fields, bike to a friend's house, and goof off in a swimming pool. My heart aches whenever I read of
a childhood plagued by cancer.

While viewing programs for St. Jude's Hospital
I am left with a desperate need to turn off the channel and ignore the suffering or to
do something.

I want my readers to know that we going to *do something!* We might not be doctors or nurses, but we can help to change the atmosphere and imagery
that a child sees from that hospital bed.

Every year, a percentage of sales from *A Picture Perfect Childhood* will go towards purchasing
new children books which will be donated to St. Jude Children's Hospital in time for the Christmas holidays.

St. Jude Children's
Research Hospital
ALSAC · Danny Thomas, Founder
Finding cures. Saving children.
1-800-996-4100
www.stjude.org

Thank you for your helping *do something*
and please continue to pray for
a cure and that these children will be
blessed with a *picture perfect childhood.*

Picture-Perfect Photo Tip

"I think he had not the slightest idea how to set about instructing a small child. My father took me on his lap...and turned the pages of a New Testament picture book, commenting briefly on the pictures as we considered them one by one. At the pictures of the passion of Christ I refused to look. I had caught a glimpse of one and that was enough. My father was understanding about this and we turned them over in a lump, leaping straight from Palm Sunday to Easter day and ignoring the crux of the matter altogether. Yet now I think that turning the pages of that picture book with my father was the most important thing that ever happened to me, important because for the first time in my life the man in the picture book came out of it and was alive...my father had in some way communicated his own conviction to me. He had made the Christ in the picture book a living person."

~ Written by English author Elizabeth Goudge in her autobiography entitled *Joy of the Snow* about her father, a professor at Oxford

If you have any requests for future booklists or would like to see a change made in *A Picture Perfect Childhood*, please email the author at:
caygibson@bellsouth.net

Stop for a visit at Cay's Cajun Cottage and sign-up for Free
Library Binder downloads and more Picture Perfect Photo
Albums for Families
http://caygibson.typepad.com

Contact Cay at caygibson@bellsouth.net

Books by Cay Gibson

Literature Alive! $35.00
A giant 300+ page book about discovering the joys of literature
with your child.

Christmas Mosaic---seasonal study guide published by
Hillside Education
(www.hillsideeducation.com)......................................$20.00

Catholic Mosaic published by Hillside Education
(www.hillsideeducation.com)

Black and White version....................$28.00
Color version............................$42.00

To receive copies, include $8.00 (S/H & Tax) and mail a check
or money order to: Cay Gibson
                        1414 Lewis St.
                        Sulphur, LA 70663

Made in the USA
Middletown, DE
29 January 2016